For agonized seconds, Burnett had no idea what to do.

After all, for the man he'd always been, there were few options at this point. He held no power over her, so he couldn't make demands.

Then it occurred to him. "Ned" was vulnerable. Ned was sensitive. Ned could do things Burnett would consider blatant displays of weakness and irresponsibility. Ned could beg, plead, throw himself at a woman's feet.... And, to Frannie Lawry, he *was* Ned.

He dropped to his knees before her, wrapped his arms around her and looked up at her, pleading with his eyes.

She stiffened. He held his breath. And he didn't allow himself to breathe again until he felt the hesitant touch of her hand.

"Oh, Ned..." She sighed. And her fingers began to comb gently through his hair....

*　　*　　*

Some readers will remember Burnett Clinton as the brother of the hero in Double Dare. *And yes, Burnett has changed—and it took an Earth Angel to bring him around.*

Dear Reader,

Happy New Year! May this year bring you happiness, good health and all you wish for. And hopefully, helping you along the way, is Silhouette **Special Edition**. Each month, Silhouette **Special Edition** publishes six novels with you in mind—stories of love and life, tales that you can identify with—romance with that little "something special" added in.

In January, don't miss love stories from Barbara Faith, Christine Rimmer, Nikki Benjamin, newcomer Susan Mallery and veteran Silhouette **Special Edition**-er, Lisa Jackson. To round out this month, you are invited to a *Wedding Party* by Patricia McLinn—the conclusion to her heartwarming *Wedding Duet*! It's a winter wonderland for all this month at Silhouette **Special Edition**!

In each Silhouette **Special Edition** novel, we're dedicated to bringing you the romances that you dream about—the type of stories that delight as well as bring a tear to the eye. And that's what Silhouette **Special Edition** is all about—special books by special authors for special readers!

I hope you enjoy this book and all of the stories to come.

Sincerely,

Tara Gavin
Senior Editor

CHRISTINE RIMMER
Earth Angel

Silhouette Special Edition

Published by Silhouette Books New York

America's Publisher of Contemporary Romance

For Downieville, always my heart's home.
And with special thanks to Matthew Reynolds,
who loves my sandwiches, brings me ice water—
and helped with the map.

SILHOUETTE BOOKS
300 East 42nd St., New York, N.Y. 10017

Books by Christine Rimmer

Silhouette Desire

No Turning Back #418
Call It Fate #458
Temporary Temptress #602
Hard Luck Lady #640

Silhouette Special Edition

Double Dare #646
Slow Larkin's Revenge #698
Earth Angel #719

CHRISTINE RIMMER,

a third generation Californian, came to her profession the long way around. Before settling down to write about the magic of romance, she'd been an actress, a sales clerk, a janitor, a model, a phone sales representative, a teacher, a waitress, a playwright and an office manager. Now that she's finally found work that suits her perfectly, she insists she never had a problem keeping a job—she was merely gaining ''life experience'' for her future as a novelist. Those who know her best withhold comment when she makes such claims; they are grateful that she's at last found steady work. Christine is grateful, too—not only for the joy she finds in writing, but for what waits when the day's work is through: a man she loves who loves her right back and the privilege of watching their children grow and change day to day.

Earth Angel is the long-awaited sequel to Christine's *Double Dare*. Readers who loved *Double Dare* did not want it to end, at least not until they found out what happened to Burnett Clinton, Casey Clinton's commanding, successful brother.

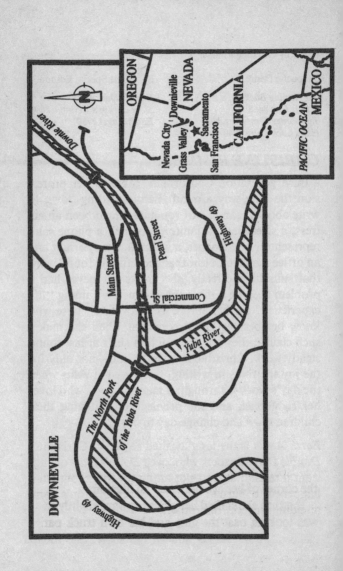

Chapter One

Out in the frozen world beyond the kitchen window, a flicker of movement caught Frannie's eye.

Curious, she approached the window. She had entered the kitchen to refill her cup of hot cider, and she'd already done that. Now she took a cautious sip. As the sweet heat slid down her throat, Frannie searched the icy landscape before her.

She scanned the clean carpet of new snow, which rolled out from under the posts that held the back of the old house above the river during flood times. At first, the pure whiteness below lay still as a held breath. Perhaps, Frannie thought, the flutter she'd seen out of the corner of her eye had been an illusion.

But then she shifted her glance upward slightly so she was looking past the gate and her own truck parked beside it, half buried now in the snow. She looked across the unpaved road that ran by the back fence. Beyond the road rose the levee, and on the other side of that, the river ran icy and swift.

At the base of the levee, Frannie saw what had moved. It was a man—there in the shadow of a cedar tree by the side of the road.

A very tattered-looking man. Even from several hundred feet away, Frannie could see that his clothes were old and worn: a pitiful plaid wool jacket, torn denim pants that probably extended to overalls beneath the jacket, and bulky brown boots. He was a big man, well over six feet.

As Frannie watched, he came out from under the shadow of the cedar tree. She could distinguish the color of his hair then; it was a deep black-brown, surprisingly rich looking, even in the flat light from the gray winter sky.

Shuffling and lurching, he began to climb the levee. The foot of snow that had fallen since dawn was still loose and powdery. It impeded his progress, imprisoning his feet with each step he took.

But Frannie suspected that the new snow wasn't the real reason the man was having such difficulty negotiating the short climb to the top of the levee. The man reeled. Frannie would have bet her favorite Christmas record that he'd spent the better part of the afternoon bending his elbow in one of the two bars on Main Street not far away.

Frannie shrugged and sipped again from her mug. The man was none of her business. In the living room at the front of the house, she'd been in the process of decorating her Christmas tree. She should get back to it.

Yet she didn't move. The man intrigued her. There was something in the set of his broad shoulders that drew her. Something determined and proud that completely contradicted his lurching walk and pitiful clothes.

With some difficulty, he made it to the top. He stood, large and tattered, silhouetted against the winter sky. He swayed on his feet for several seconds, and then seemed to gather himself to stand tall.

He took something from his rear pocket—probably a wallet, Frannie decided, because he paused, his body swaying once again, to fiddle with it for a moment. Then he shoved his hand into the side pocket of the old jacket, as if sticking something from the presumed wallet in there.

That action almost cost him his balance—he teetered like a falling tree. Frannie smiled in spite of herself, and then felt her smile melt away. He was sad and silly. And yet there remained that other quality, which was serious and solemn and full of noble purpose.

Once again, he collected himself and slid his free hand to his breast beneath the jacket. He pulled his hand out again, clutching something flat and palm-sized.

For a moment he was very still, arms at his sides, looking out over the surging gray river before him. The quality of grave determination that Frannie had sensed in him seemed suddenly stronger than before. His big shoulders were set, his head high.

Frannie felt a little catch in her throat, a quick thrill of fear. Could he be thinking of tossing himself out into the rushing water? Was she standing sipping cider at her window, witnessing a man attempting to end his life?

Slowly, with great and somber dignity, the man raised his hands straight out to his sides, still clutching in each fist the objects he'd found in his clothes. He rocked, his body swaying toward the river.

"No!" Frannie heard herself gasp, sure in that moment that he intended to hurl his body into the pounding torrent below. She slammed her mug on the counter, slopping cider across the ancient Formica, and reached for the window latch. The latch was old and stubborn. She struggled with it.

Sounds of frustration escaped her. She had to get the window open, call out to him, beg him to reconsider. True, life could seem a pointless thing, each day a wasteland, each night an eternity where the best you could hope for was just to get through it—to face another meaningless day. But even the emptiest of lives could be turned around. It had happened for Frannie Lawry. It could happen for the raggedy man on the levee, she knew that it could!

Frannie glanced up from her struggle with the window—and her fingers stopped fighting the latch. She watched, unmoving, as the man flung the objects in his hands, one at a time, into the river below. That done, he planted his fists on his hips and stared at the river once more. His entire stance shouted grim satisfaction as the river carried away whatever it was he'd tossed into it.

He showed no inclination whatsoever to throw himself in next.

Frannie let go of the window latch, feeling more than a little foolish. The man was no potential suicide. He was just a poor guy on a bender, behaving oddly, throwing the contents of his pockets into the river for reasons he himself would probably wonder about when he finally sobered up. He was a total stranger, doing nothing threatening to anybody—not even himself. His actions should be no concern of Frannie's.

She cast an irritated glance at her spilled cider, and started to reach for the counter sponge. But the man was turning around now and starting back down the levee. Once again, Frannie found herself observing his unsteady progress.

He didn't get far. Two steps down the slope, his legs shot out from under him. He went sliding on his backside, plowing the powdery snow as he went. He landed at the base of the levee, faceup to the lowering sky.

Once he stopped sliding, he didn't move.

Frannie waited for him to stir. He remained utterly still.

There was really no reason to be concerned about him, Frannie told herself. He was just—resting for a moment, before he dragged himself to his feet and went on his way.

From the front of the house she could hear the festive sounds of the Christmas carols she'd been playing while she trimmed her tree.

Halfway through a chorus of "Jingle Bells," the man still hadn't moved. But of course, he would get up soon enough. She should get back to the tree and her private holiday celebration.

Yet she didn't. She kept watching him, thinking vaguely that as soon as he stirred and she knew he was all right, she would turn and forget about him once and for all.

As the seconds stretched out, Frannie became aware of the popping sounds made by the fire in the cast-iron stove a few feet away. She heard the muffled crunch of a log collapsing within. She smelled the tart sweetness of the steam escaping from the pan of cider on top.

She remembered the spilled cider on the counter, turned, picked up the sponge and mopped it up.

That done, she shot a look out the window again. The man was perfectly still, spread-eagled, like someone who'd been staked out to die there, in the snow.

Frannie made a low, disgusted sound in her throat. She just had to stop imagining tragic things about him. He was no victim. He was just a drunk who had passed out in the snow. And if he didn't get up in a little while, someone would go down there and help him. He was in plain sight of other houses than Frannie's, so eventually someone else would notice him and do something about him—someone other than a single woman staying alone.

She glanced at the wood basket beside the stove. It was almost empty, just a few sticks of kindling and one lone pine log left. She might as well refill it before returning to the front of the house.

Resolutely veering from the window and the sight of the inert figure at the bottom of the levee, Frannie took the heavy work gloves that were hung on the side of the basket and then headed for the basement stairs.

When she reached the foot of the stairs, where the cut wood was stacked neatly against the dirt wall that supported the front of the house, she reminded herself that her kindling supply was low. Tomorrow she'd make time to split some.

The door to the one finished room beneath the house was slightly ajar. She'd left it that way after lunch, when she came down to get the box of decorations stored in there. Frannie pulled the door closed and then put on the heavy gloves.

She made three trips up and down to refill the basket. Each time she entered the kitchen, she was scrupulously careful not to let her glance stray toward the window. When at last the box was full of wood, she removed her gloves and laid them on the rim of the basket again.

Now she would turn and march back through the dining room to the living room, where another fire crackled in the grate and her tree stood proudly before the front window, already strung with lights and ready for some serious bulb-hanging. All she needed was her cider. She strode past the window to reach it—and, in her peripheral vision, saw that dingy plaid jacket again.

Sighing, Frannie turned and once more stared at the motionless figure still sprawled in the snow.

How long had he been lying there now? Ten minutes, maybe?

And how cold was it out there, actually? And how long till dark—a half hour or so?

She allowed herself to wonder if, beyond being drunk, he might be hurt or ill?

Frances, a cynical voice in her mind rebuked, *must you romanticize even an insensible drunk?*

Though it was only in her mind, Frannie recognized the voice. Kenneth's. He'd dominated her life for so many years, that in moments of indecision she still imagined him pronouncing his opinions in that haughty, preemptive way of his.

The voice continued, cold and full of mounting disdain, *There's nothing wrong with that lowlife out there that a trip to a detox unit wouldn't cure. That man is not ill, except in that he's poisoned himself with alcohol. That is his responsibility. Let him live with it.*

Outside in the snow, the raggedy man lay unmoving. By dark, it would be getting even colder. The weather forecast was for more snow and a low in the mid-twenties.

Maybe she *should* go down there and—

Are you insane, *Frances?* Kenneth's imaginary voice cut her off before she could finish her thought. *The man is obviously a bum. Notify the sheriff if the sight of him bothers you, but there is absolutely no reason to become involved yourself....*

Frannie lifted her chin. She and Kenneth had parted a year and a half ago. Their divorce had been final for over six months. She was no longer the child bride of a successful older man. At thirty-three, she was her own independent person at last. What Kenneth Dayton might have thought in this situation didn't matter.

What mattered was what Frannie Lawry thought—and just what she intended to do about it.

The man, whoever or whatever he was, had been lying too still for too long. Who was to say he wouldn't get frostbite—or worse—before one of the neighbors became concerned enough to check on him?

Frannie needed to do something. Unfortunately, since she used the old house left her by her dad only for holidays and vacations, she didn't keep a phone here.

Of course, she could trudge next door to borrow her Aunt Bonnie's phone. But that prospect didn't fill her with enthusiasm. She and her aunt seemed to be forever disagreeing on things lately. They'd parted this very morning on a sour note. Now Bonnie would be full of her own opinions about what to do concerning the man in the snow.

The other option was to troop on out the back gate and rescue her raggedy man on her own.

A small chuckle escaped her. How strange. Thinking of the poor man as *hers*. Of course, he was nothing of the kind.

But he did need help.

Frannie whirled from the window and made for the side door, pausing only to lift her red down jacket off its hook on her way out.

Chapter Two

"Can you hear me?" a gentle voice asked.

Though it caused him considerable discomfort, Burnett Clinton opened an eye and willed the world to come into focus. What he saw made him force the other eye open, too.

An angel hovered above him. She had pale skin and shell-pink lips, and her dark brows were drawn together with concern.

Her hair was another story, not angelic at all, Burnett thought. She had hair that cried out to be spread on a pillow. Thick, wild, long, curly hair. It was chestnut-brown.

"Are you injured?" she asked.

Her eyes were blue. A very light blue at the center, with dark blue rims around the iris. The dark rims made the light centers somehow mesmerizing, Burnett thought.

Amanda, Burnett's ex-wife, had blue eyes. But Amanda's eyes were a uniform, flawless blue. Not an odd, arresting contrast between light and dark the way this woman's were.

"I went for a walk," Burnett told the angel, with a dignity that he himself found amazing, considering his position, sprawled faceup in the snow. "I thought the cold air might sober me up a little."

"I see," she said.

"But I fell in this snowbank, and then... I didn't get up."

"I saw you from my kitchen window." Her warm breath came out on a silvery plume. "I thought maybe you were ill."

"No, just drunk." He shook his head, which caused all manner of minor explosions in his brain. Then he added, feeling defiant, "And it's not even dark yet." Truth to tell, Burnett Clinton could never remember being drunk in his whole life, let alone so drunk he could topple into a snowbank at five in the afternoon and not be able to get up.

Beyond the chestnut halo of the angel's wild hair, the pewter winter sky seemed to vibrate. Burnett's stomach churned. He closed his eyes once more, hoping that when he dared open them again, the world would stop pulsing in rhythm with the pounding in his head.

He felt someone pulling on his arm. "Come on," the angel urged, "Let me help you."

She was strong, for an angel, and she managed to get him to a sitting position before he knew what was happening. He opened his eyes again.

The harsh winter light found its way to his pounding brain. It hurt—both having his eyes open, and sitting up.

"No, no," he shook his head—a mistake because it intensified the pounding. "I'm too disgusting." With a groan, he fell back upon the blanket of white, shut his eyes and turned his cheek against the icy coldness.

"You can't just lie here," she said.

"Watch me."

"Please, Mr..."

He realized she was waiting for a name. He wished he was someone else, anyone but Burnett Clinton, a man who'd sunk so low that he couldn't drag himself out of a snowbank on his own steam.

"Ned," Burnett heard himself say. "Call me Ned." His first name was Edward, after the father he'd hated, and everyone used to call him Ned years ago, until he'd grown old enough to reject the name and adopt his middle name, Burnett, as his own.

"Do you have a last name, Ned?" the angel asked.

A last name. Did he have a last name? He thought of the bar he'd recently staggered from, the St. Charles Place bar. "St. Charles," he said. "Ned St. Charles."

"Ned St. Charles," the angel said. The name sounded wonderful on her lips. "Please let me help you. The temperature's dropping. It'll be dark soon, and it's going to snow again, too."

"I could freeze to death," he said matter-of-factly, keeping his eyes clenched shut. Right then, freezing didn't seem like such a terrible fate. If he froze to death he wouldn't have to live through the hangover he was going to be experiencing soon.

"I doubt you'll be allowed to freeze," she said, her voice suddenly tart. "You're in plain sight of the Riverside Motel, as well as half the houses on Commercial Street. Someone will come down and pull you out soon enough—probably the sheriff."

"Oh." Burnett pondered this information.

"In fact, since you're too big for me to carry, maybe it's better if I go hunt down someone larger to help you up."

He heard the crunching of the snow as she rose from her kneeling position beside him.

His angel was leaving him.

"Wait!" he said, oblivious to the ringing echo the word set off in his aching brain. He opened his eyes and lifted his head off its pillow of snow.

She towered above him, miles away, incredibly beautiful. She had her hands stuck into the pockets of the red jacket she was wearing. "What is it, Ned St. Charles?"

"You came down here. To help me. You don't even know what kind of guy I am. People don't do things like that anymore."

"This is Downieville," she said. "It's a small town. People help each other here. It's understood."

"Oh," he said.

"I'll be back soon. Don't worry," she assured him, starting to turn away.

"Wait!" he said again.

She stopped. "What?"

He gazed at her for a moment, his mind a blank. Then words finally came to him. "Today's the day my divorce is final."

"I'm sorry," she said.

He let his head fall back, but held on to her bewitching gaze. "No," he told his angel. "That marriage was no good. I couldn't give her what she wanted. And maybe I never really loved her anyway. She was perfect. She was exactly what I thought I should want. But we were never happy. I don't think I know how...to be happy."

The angel said nothing, she just looked at him, her head tipped in an attitude of listening.

Beyond the levee behind him, Burnett could hear the river's hollow roar. "Why am I telling you this?" he said at last.

She shrugged, her slim shoulders lifting and dropping in that blindingly red jacket. "Maybe you need someone to talk to."

"But I don't want to talk about it. I want to forget about it."

"Fine," she said. Then, "I'll be back soon."

"No, please." He just couldn't let her walk away.

"Yes?"

"Don't leave me here for the snow to fall on."

She smiled then. The smile lit up her already incredible face. Burnett's stricken senses reeled.

"Then you're going to help me?" she asked.

"Help you what?"

"I'll need you to work with me to get you up. You're a pretty big man. I'm strong, but I doubt if I can do it unless you help."

Burnett considered her words. Then he said, momentously solemn, "I am going to help you to help me. Indubiously."

She actually laughed. Her laughter was like bells. "You mean indubitably."

"Right. Absolutely." He managed to nod—with great dignity, he thought.

"All right, Ned," she said. He wondered for a moment who Ned was, and then he remembered that *he* was Ned. He'd always been Ned; he'd just made everyone call him Burnett for the last twenty-seven years of his life.

It had been a mistake, he realized now, to have ever changed his name. Burnett Clinton had lived an empty, meaningless life. Burnett Clinton was rich. Burnett Clinton had everything—except love and laughter and someone to call his own.

He supposed, if he were fair, that he must admit his family loved him—his mother and his brother and his brother's wife and his little nephew, Mike. They loved him *in spite* of how difficult he'd made it for them to love him. To them, he was someone who insisted on making them all rich—whether they really wanted to be rich or not—and then tried to run their lives. He was someone they put up with because they understood that he *meant* well.

His angel had swooped down to his level again. She grabbed his hand in her slim one, and yanked him up to a sitting position once more. He heard a groan, and realized it came from him.

"Lord, that hurts," he said.

"Your arm?" she asked, since that was what she'd been pulling on.

"Everything. My stomach, my head, my eyebrows, my hair..."

"You should have considered that earlier," she muttered dryly.

"I've been a fool," he said with becoming gravity.

She said nothing, only wrapped his arm around her slim shoulders and then wedged herself against his side.

"Okay," she told him. "Let's get you to a crouch first. Pull up your knees and put your feet flat on the ground." She waited while he did that. "Now, when I say the word, you rock up onto your feet."

He could feel the warmth of her all along his side. It was wonderful. He hadn't realized how damn cold it was until right then.

Lightly, the snow began to fall again. Big, fat flakes drifted down. They fell on his angel's unruly hair and melted on her dark brows.

"What's your name?" he asked.

"Frances. Call me Frannie. You ready?"

"As I'll ever be."

"Oomph," they said in unison, and Burnett found himself kneeling on his feet.

"Halfway there," she told him. "Okay, when I say now…" He took in a breath, and held it. "Now!" she said.

The breath he'd drawn came out in a hard rush as, with a superhuman effort and the help of his angel, Burnett surged to his full height.

Being upright was not a pleasant experience. The world went spinning. He staggered.

"Whoa…" she said, and steadied him.

Burnett sucked in another breath and let it out with great care. His surroundings ceased whirling crazily and settled into a slow, stomach-churning slide.

"We did it," she announced, her soft voice full of pride.

Burnett said nothing; he was trying not to disgrace himself all over his angel's red parka.

"Now," she went on. "Ned, where did you come from?"

. He swallowed, forced himself to think. Where did he come from? He remembered.

"The bar."

She shook her head, her hair picking up static against the scratchy wool of the ancient jacket he wore. "No," she tried again, "I mean, where do you live? You aren't from town, are you?"

He considered. Where did he live? *Burnett* lived in Sacramento, in a big house off of Fair Oaks Boulevard.

"Town?" he asked.

"From here, Downieville," she elaborated, with a look that said she wondered if he'd actually managed to do some permanent damage to his brain.

"No, not from town," he said.

"Where, then?"

Then it came to him. The cabin in Graeagle. Where he'd gone to be alone. His family's cabin, where he'd found the disgraceful clothes he was wearing in a dusty box upstairs and put them on because...why? It was something about wishing he were someone else. Anyone else but Burnett Clinton who had it all, and still had nothing.

"Ned?" his angel prompted again. "Can't you tell me where you're from."

Where I'm from, he thought. "Graeagle," he said.

"Graeagle? But that's up past the summit, through the Lakes Basin."

"Right. I went for a drive this morning. I ended up here." She was giving him an exasperated look. He attempted a shrug and explained as if it were worth something, "The bar was open."

"Yes." Her tone was wry. "I think we've already established that."

She was quiet for a moment—trying to decide what to do with him, no doubt. He experimented with squinting his eyes, to see if the houses across the road would stop moving around so much.

"Well," she said finally, "you'll have to check into the motel, then. The roads are going to be rough going tonight—and it would be illegal for you to drive in your condition anyway." Her breath, scented faintly of apples and cinnamon, was warm against his cold cheek.

She was tall for an angel, he realized, only four or five inches shorter than his own six-three. He liked that. No wimpy little dinky angels for Burnett Clinton—correction, Ned St. Charles—no sirree.

"Ned? Did you hear me?"

"Um. Yes. Every word."

"We're just going to struggle down this road here, okay? I'll take you to the motel."

Burnett remembered what he'd recently done with his wallet and his money clip. All he had in his pockets now was his driver's license. He'd saved that because, even so drunk he could barely stand, the solid citizen inside him couldn't bear the thought of walking around without identification. If it really became necessary, he'd wanted the means to prove who he was on demand.

"Ned? Are you phasing out on me again?"

"'Scuse me?"

"I said we're going to walk to the motel now."

He shook his head. "So sorry. Can't do that."

"Yes, you can," she said gently. "I'll help you."

"No, not that. I don't mean I can't walk. I can walk, more or less."

"What is it, then?" she asked.

He looked at her very seriously, drawing his brows together, but forgot to say anything.

"Why can't you go to the motel?" his angel prompted.

He understood he needed to answer then. "No money," he said gravely.

"No money," she repeated after him. She said it more as a confirmation than a question, and she didn't sound the least surprised.

"Not a red cent," he announced with an absurd flare of pride. Of course, even in his inebriated state, he knew it would take no more than a single phone call to line his pockets once again. But he wasn't going to tell his angel that.

To her, he was Ned St. Charles, from Graeagle. A pitiful case. A loser at the game of life. Ned St. Charles had hit rock bottom. He was the kind of guy God just might send an angel to help.

Burnett Clinton needed help, too. But God, rightfully, wouldn't worry about him. Burnett Clinton had everything. It wasn't God's problem if Burnett Clinton couldn't make himself happy.

"Not even a credit card?" his angel asked.

"Threw my wallet in the river," he replied.

"Why?"

"I had this crazy idea that money meant nothing," he told her.

Her haunting eyes shifted once, and he knew she was thinking that there couldn't have been much in the wallet to begin with. It was logical that she'd come to that conclusion, given his condition and the old clothes he was wearing.

She was watching him, her head against his shoulder as her body helped to brace him upright. Her magical eyes gazed into his. It occurred to him that anyone glancing at them from a nearby house might think they were lovers out for a stroll, cuddled up close against the winter cold. Burnett smiled at the thought; it held definite appeal.

She saw his smile and became stern. "So you have no money."

"Nope." Well, he didn't—not *on* him.

"And nowhere to go."

"Right." Or at least, nowhere that mattered.

"What in the world am I going to do with you?"

He tried to look as appealing as possible—given the circumstances. "Take me home?"

Her strange eyes narrowed at him. "Give me a good reason why I should take a drunk stranger into my house."

"Pity?" he tried.

She was silent.

"It's Christmastime," he reminded her hopefully.

She shook her head.

He said a word he'd rarely uttered in his thirty-eight years. "Please."

She was silent again. He held his breath. At last, she said warily, "All right. I do have a room in my basement..."

"A room," he said, still hardly daring to breathe. Somewhere warm to lie down, he was thinking. A place where, when he woke up tomorrow, she'd be there.

That seemed even more important than a warm bed to pass out in right now—to make sure she would still be there when morning dawned. Having found his angel at last, he had to be careful she didn't fly away.

"I suppose you could stay there," she offered. "For this one night. To sleep it off." Her voice was reluctant.

"Yes, to sleep it off," he said too eagerly.

Her eyes narrowed further. When she spoke, it was in a warning tone. "There's a deadbolt lock on the door between the basement and the house," she told him. "I plan to use it."

He looked at her seriously, and slowly assimilated that she was telling him that her door would be locked against him, should he have any sinister plans.

"Fine," he said.

She didn't look completely convinced. She glared at him measuringly, and then pointed to one of the houses opposite where they stood on the snow-covered road. "See that house right there?"

He squinted where she pointed. "You bet."

"See that woman looking out the kitchen window?"

He saw the outline of a head in the window she was pointing to. "I see someone," he allowed.

"That's my aunt, Bonnie Lawry. The house to the left of hers is mine."

"Oh," he said, not sure what she was getting at.

"What I'm saying is, Aunt Bonnie's seen you. If I take you to my house, there'd better not be any funny stuff. Because she'll know you were there."

Burnett wondered, with some irony, exactly what Aunt Bonnie would *do* were he to commit some transgression. By the time she found out, it would be too late. He opened his mouth to inform his angel that the threat of her Aunt Bonnie's wrath probably wouldn't add up to much if he were really intent on *funny stuff*. But then it occurred to him that such a remark wouldn't help his case much.

He raised the hand that wasn't slung over Frannie's shoulder. "I swear. No funny stuff," he said. Even if he were the type of man prone to funny stuff, he was in no condition for it. In his current state, he'd be lucky to stagger to the basement room his angel had offered him and collapse on the first piece of furniture that presented itself.

She was looking at him doubtfully, shaking her head. "I've got to be out of my mind," she sighed.

"No," he said, "not out of your mind at all."

"Then what?"

He considered, and the answer came. "You're good. A good person. Generous and kind." And an angel, he added silently. *My* angel. At last.

She smiled just a little. "Thanks."

"Welcome."

They looked at each other for a moment through the thickening fall of the snow. Then her gaze slid away, and she gestured at the house she'd said was hers. "Let's get started. There's a basement entrance, so it won't be too far."

"Ah," Burnett said, nodding. He looked where she pointed, and tried to estimate the distance he was going to have to walk.

The distance was rather hard to judge, actually. The snow was falling harder, like a softly swirling veil between himself and the white clapboard structure that she had pointed to. And, of course, there was the cruel glitter of the snow on the ground to further confuse him, not to mention the way stationary objects just refused to *stay* stationary. Everything rippled and swayed. Except his angel. She was warm and firm— and yet soft at the same time—braced at his side.

She took a step.

His stomach lurched. "Oh, God," he said. "I can't do this."

"One foot in front of the other," she told him.

"Oh, God," he said again, and they started across the road.

She took him, one stomach-churning step at a time, across the road. They had to stagger around a parked truck to reach the gate. Once through the gate, they lurched past a lot of bare bushes sticking up through the fiercely brilliant snow. When they reached the house, they went beneath an overhang between supporting posts. She guided him around the side, to where there was a rough wooden door with a padlock on it.

"Rest here." She propped him up against the wall and removed the lock, which had only been turned but not engaged.

He thought to reprimand her for not keeping it locked. She was much too trusting, he decided. Leaving her doors open, taking in strange men she found in the snow. But then the door swung open, creaking loud enough, it seemed, to make his head explode, and he knew right then that if he tried to lecture her, he would be sick.

"Come on." She hooked his arm around her shoulder, and bolstered him once more. They stepped down into the dark basement, which was as cold as it was outside and smelled of frozen earth.

Burnett felt the contents of his stomach rise up alarmingly. He distracted himself from the certainty that he was going to be sick by exerting a superhuman effort to study his surroundings.

They tottered across a concrete floor, past stacks of firewood on one side and a washer and dryer that had seen a lot of loads on the other. They stopped where the concrete ended.

He paused, swaying. "Oh, no. Stairs," he groaned.

"Only four steps," she reassured him. "To that door there."

"Oh, no," he said again, but she was already guiding him upward.

He managed—Lord knew how—to negotiate those four steps. They stopped at a small landing in front of the door she'd mentioned. To their left, the stairs turned and continued up—to the main house, he presumed.

His angel pushed open the door in front of them. He saw a low-ceilinged cell of a room with a window on the outside wall, a battered chest, a closet—and a single bed.

Nothing in his life had ever looked as wonderful as that bed. His weary body yearned for it.

They made it up the last step and over the threshold. His head grazed the low ceiling as she helped him stagger to the bed and sink down upon it.

"Now, don't you dare lie down yet," she said. She'd dropped to the bed with him, and was still tucked beneath his arm, keeping him from doing what he most longed to do—fall over on his side. "We've got to get your coat and boots off," she continued. "But first I want to turn the heater on."

"Yes, ma'am," he humbly replied, and then found himself grinning, almost forgetting that if he didn't stretch out flat he would probably die.

He wished his brother could have heard him say *yes, ma'am* like that. Casey would never believe Burnett capable of sounding so meek and obedient unless he heard it with his own ears.

"What's so funny?" his angel was asking.

"My brother, Casey," he said without thinking, "would not believe what a mess I'm in now."

She pulled away from him and stood looking down at him. Her eyes looked sad. He could see she felt sorry for him, for pitiful Ned whose life was out of control. "You're often in trouble, then?" she asked.

He couldn't speak for a moment as he looked up into her face. God, she was beautiful. Her pale skin seemed to glow. He thought it was about time he told her who he really was. But then, who was he—really? Ned *was* his real first name, and he *had* come from Graeagle. Calling himself Ned *St. Charles* might have been pushing it a little too far...

"Ned?" she asked, concerned at his extended silence.

Hell, he thought. I'm drunk. I can't explain it all now. Plenty of time for that later, when I'm sober, when I can lay it all out for her, in simple, clear terms.

She was looking worried. He realized he needed to say something. To answer her question...what was the question?

He remembered—was he often in trouble? That was what she had asked.

How to answer that—without lying, exactly, but without having to explain everything right now when he just wasn't in any condition to explain.

How, he found himself wondering, would Ned answer that question?

Ned was on the skids—but he still had his pride. And Ned was every bit as drunk as Burnett was right at the moment.

So, he decided, Ned wouldn't want to take on the question of the trouble he'd been in any more than Burnett did. But how would Ned avoid it?

He thought of a manager he'd been forced to fire—a once-dependable fellow who hadn't been able to pull himself together after a series of personal setbacks. The day Burnett had let him go, the man wouldn't look at him. He'd been silent and withdrawn, the few things he did say hesitant and unsure. Perhaps Ned was like that...

Burnett looked away from his angel. "In our family, Casey was the wild one," he said, telling the truth about his younger brother. "And I was the *good* boy. But lately..." He didn't finish, as if it was just too painful to go on.

He heard her soft sigh. "Never mind. I guess now's not the time to go into that anyway."

He glanced back at her, putting on a brave smile. She smiled in return, and his heart did something strange inside his chest. He felt himself swaying, and quickly braced his fists to either side.

She put up a hand. "Don't fall over yet."

Then she whirled, so quick and lithe he had to close his eyes to keep his head from spinning. He heard an electric whine and realized she'd switched on a portable heater against the inside wall opposite where he sat. He felt the heat from it immediately in the small space.

Then she was back in front of him, busy and purposeful, making his brain reel from the force of her sheer, focused energy as she pushed the old coat off his shoulders.

He tried to be helpful, he really did. But the minute he lifted one fist off the bed, he crumpled to that side and lay there, bent at the waist, his face smashed into the nubby softness of the pink bedspread.

"Oh, well," he heard her sigh. "I'll get the one side off while it's easy to get at." She made a few soft little noises as she worked the jacket off of his left side. And then she pulled on his arm to try to get him upright again. He felt himself being lifted, his cheek leaving the soft, tufted spread for a moment.

But then he must have been too heavy. She let him back down. He heard a moan, and barely recognized it as his own. As it had out in the snow when he landed at the base of the levee, the soft, blessed void of unconsciousness enticed him. It was like a warm pool of darkness, a place he could drown in and forget everything for a while.

But then his angel was pushing at him from the other side, until she got him sitting again. He hung there, and then toppled the other way. He felt the jacket leave him.

And then she was levering his legs up on the bed. His booted feet hung off the end. He remembered, for some inexplicable reason, his custom-made bed at home. It was a super king-size and extra-long, so that he could sleep on his back and have all of him on the bed.

Home, his foggy mind scoffed. Was that empty showplace of a house he owned really anything that remotely resembled a home? Even Amanda, who had done most of the decorating herself, hadn't wanted to live there in the end.

"It's much too traditional," she had said. "After all, I chose every last stick of furniture with you in mind." There had been that tone of noble reproach. "No, darling, I'll take my share in money. Ashford prefers a more contemporary style." Ashford was the man Amanda lived with now, a lawyer. He'd had eight children and a lovely wife when Amanda had met him. Now, since Amanda was pregnant, he was about to have nine children—and a *new* wife, as soon as his own divorce was final next month.

"Now, the boots," he heard his angel say. He forgot all about Amanda and Ashford as he felt nimble fingers working the laces, and then, at last, pulling the boots off his feet.

He heard her step away. The closet door opened and closed. And then a heavy quilt that smelled faintly of mothballs settled over him. It was big enough that she could tuck it in beneath his stockinged feet. She said something like, "I'll bring down a big bowl, just in case..." He managed to nod, vaguely understanding that he was to use the bowl should his stomach rebel in the night.

Burnett sighed, and, even as blackness beckoned again, he felt his cold body warming and thought that it was good. "Wonderful. Thank you," he mumbled, and covered his eyes with his arm.

She might have said, "you're welcome" but he wasn't sure, because unconsciousness was coming at him like a huge wave, rising up and tumbling over him. He surrendered to it, as he had never in his life surrendered to anything, passing into oblivion like a swimmer swallowed by a midnight sea.

He didn't see her turn and leave, nor was he aware of her return with the promised bowl. Neither did he observe the way she hovered at his side, her mouth turning suddenly soft and tender. He also missed the flush of excitement that chased the softness away.

Beyond that, he didn't hear the way her breath caught when she realized what she'd been thinking. And he didn't see her whirl and flee the room, barely pausing to drop the bowl by the bed and whip the door closed behind her.

Chapter Three

Her breath coming too rapidly into her chest, Frannie turned the deadbolt that effectively sealed off the basement from the rest of the house.

She shivered, though the fire in the stove kept the kitchen toasty-warm. What in the world had she let herself imagine down there?

The sound of knuckles tapping on glass across the room saved her from having to answer her own question right then. She collected her scattered wits and turned for the side door, which was set with small glass panes in the top half. Through the panes, Bonnie Lawry's sharp dark eyes peered at her.

Putting her private thoughts away, Frannie went to let her aunt in from the cold. Since the shadows of twilight had darkened the high-ceilinged room, Frannie flipped on the light switch as she pulled open the door.

The two women regarded each other for a moment, and then Bonnie began busily brushing snow from her bare head, and stomping it off of her rubber boots onto the mat. That done, she stepped inside so Frannie could close the door.

The two stood close together. Bonnie leveled a piercing look at her niece. "I thought I should at least check on you," she said, "after I saw you pull that strange man from the snow."

Frannie looked away. "I'm fine, Aunt Bonnie." She busied herself shrugging out of her own red jacket and hanging it on the peg beside the door. That done, she held out her hand. "Here. Let me take your coat."

"No, I'll just keep it on." Bonnie wrapped her plump arms around herself and gave a shiver. Frannie felt guiltily relieved, thinking that if she wouldn't take off her coat, perhaps her aunt didn't plan to stay long enough to start asking uncomfortable questions. But then Bonnie sniffed. "What's that delicious smell?"

"Hot cider," Frannie allowed, then paused. Her aunt's bright eyes burned through her, and Frannie's ingrained good manners won out over her desire to avoid the coming interrogation. She asked, with a touch of irony, "Won't you have a cup?"

"Why, thank you, dear." Bonnie now looked quite serene. "Shall I get it myself?"

"No, no," Frannie said, handing out the rote courtesies more elaborately than necessary. "You sit down. Make yourself at home."

"Thank you. I shall."

Bonnie went to the scarred walnut table in the center of the room and pulled out a chair. Frannie opened a cupboard, saying no more, waiting for her aunt to begin asking the questions that Frannie knew would come.

Bonnie kept her peace until Frannie had poured the last of the cider into a mug, set it before her, and carried the pan to the sink. Then she asked, suddenly brusque, "Well, then, what did you do with him?"

Frannie ran water into the pan. "I put him to bed in the basement."

"He's down there now?"

"Yes, he is." Frannie glanced over her shoulder in time to see Bonnie shoot a look at the basement door. "It's locked," Frannie assured her.

"I should hope so."

Frannie flipped off the tap and went to sit in the chair at the head of the table. "I also told him that you knew what he looked like. So if he tried anything, he'd live to regret it."

Bonnie clucked her tongue. "I'll just bet that terrified him."

"Aunt Bonnie, he's harmless."

"Why do you think that? Because he told you so?"

"No, I just, well, I just know it."

"Ah, you've recently become psychic?"

Frannie looked away, and then back again. "He's staying the night. I said he could and I won't go back on my word."

Bonnie sipped from her cider and looked out the window at the darkness and the snow for a moment. "Has he got a name?"

"Ned. St. Charles."

"St. Charles?" Bonnie scoffed. "What kind of name is that for a man?"

"There's nothing wrong with it."

"It sounds phony."

"It does not."

"And it's also suspicious. Think about it. There's that big marker over town, where the St. Charles hotel once stood—not to mention that it's the name of one of the bars. It's just the kind of thing a drunk up to no good would do—give a name he's recently seen on a window somewhere instead of saying who he really is."

"Oh, Aunt Bonnie. That's ridiculous. St. Charles is a perfectly acceptable name. You're just looking for any excuse to get me to put the poor man out in the cold."

"Mark my words. He made it up."

"I mean it, Aunt Bonnie. Stop it, now."

Bonnie subsided against the straight back of her chair, crossing her arms over her full bosom. She studied her niece, her head tipped to the side, like a bantam hen seeking a new place to peck.

During the brief silence that ensued, Frannie told herself that her aunt's opinion about Ned would naturally be biased. Bonnie was "an old maid, and proud of it," as she defined herself. She lived alone, and would never allow a strange man to sleep the night in her house. Besides that, Bonnie hadn't talked to Ned the way Frannie had, or seen the lonely sadness in his dark eyes.

Yes, Frannie found herself thinking. Ned did have fine eyes. There was a sensitivity in them that even his being so drunk couldn't completely mask.

"Frances, what are you thinking?" Bonnie suddenly demanded, apparently having decided that the silence had lasted long enough.

"Nothing important," Frannie answered right away.

"Are you sure? All at once, you began to look positively moony."

"I'm sure."

Bonnie narrowed her eyes suspiciously, and then decided to return to the original topic. "All right, answer me this. Just where is this Ned St. Charles from?"

"Graeagle."

Frannie was granted a look of utter disdain. "There are no people named St. Charles in Graeagle."

"Oh, Aunt Bonnie. How can you be sure of that?"

"I have lived in these parts all my life."

"You don't even know anyone who lives in Graeagle."

"Of course I do. I know several people from Graeagle—and none of them are named St. Charles."

"Aunt Bonnie, no matter what you say," Frannie stated slowly and with great care, "I'm not kicking him out tonight. He's a poor guy with a lot of problems and he tried forgetting them in the bar. He's run out of money and has no place else to go."

Frannie decided against mentioning that Ned had thrown what little cash he possessed in the river, although it was entirely possible that Bonnie had seen him do it. If her aunt asked about it, Frannie would be honest. But Frannie had no intention of volunteering the information. Bonnie would only see it as more proof that Ned should be booted out the door post-haste.

"There are many people with problems in the world, Frances," her aunt was saying in her most patient voice. "Do you plan to let them all spend the night at your house?"

"No," Frannie told her. "Just this one."

"It is foolish and dangerous."

"My mind is made up."

"Change it."

"No."

"Frances—"

"I mean it, Aunt Bonnie. He is going nowhere tonight."

Bonnie glared and fumed. "You're being as foolishly obstinate about this as you've always been about working things out with your mother," she muttered in disgust.

At that, Frannie decided she'd had enough. Earlier in the day they'd been arguing about that subject, and Frannie had told her aunt in no uncertain terms that her relationship with her mother was her own business. "Ned St. Charles stays," she said after a heavy pause, her voice hard as rock. "I absolutely refuse to kick the poor man out." Frannie took a breath, then added honestly, as she'd learned to do in the past eighteen months, "And I resent the reference to my problems with my mother."

Bonnie's pugnacious expression slackened. She was caught off-guard by the new forthrightness in her niece. Beyond that, she seemed to realize that she'd gone too far. "I apologize for bringing Alicia into this," she nobly intoned. "That is a subject for another time." She even uncrossed her arms and tried to look sheepish. But she hadn't given up the battle over where Ned St. Charles would be spending the night. Frannie knew her aunt's quick mind was ticking away, conceiving the next line of attack.

When Bonnie spoke again, she had assumed a wounded expression. "I won't sleep a wink, worrying over you all night." She took a small, pained sip of cider.

Frannie said softly, "That's emotional blackmail, Aunt Bonnie. And it isn't going to work."

Bonnie huffed, "Emotional blackmail, indeed. Where did you get that, in that support group of yours down in Sacramento?"

"Maybe, but it doesn't matter where I got it." Frannie had joined the group when she left Kenneth. Just having a regular forum to discuss what she was going through had been invaluable. "What matters is that I believe you're using emotional blackmail on me right now."

"Oh, and don't you know everything lately," Bonnie muttered, suddenly finding the lights across the river of great interest.

"Aunt Bonnie—" Frannie tried. Bonnie stopped her with a curt wave of her hand, which she then let fall to the edge of the table. Frannie covered the hand with her own and pushed on. "Do you disapprove of my support group, is that what you're trying to tell me?"

"No." Bonnie was still looking out the window, but she didn't pull her hand out from under Frannie's. "I'm sure it's good for you. It's only..." Silence fell again.

"Go on," Frannie prompted.

Bonnie's eyes, full of confusion and concern, looked into Frannie's at last. "You're different, dear."

"Yes..." Frannie smiled. "I am."

"You're so... opinionated, lately."

"Thank you."

Bonnie groaned. "That was not a compliment."

"To me it was."

"Oh my, I just don't understand you."

"I think you do, Aunt Bonnie. I think you understand me just fine."

"What is that supposed to mean?"

"Only that you are a very strong person. And that I am becoming that way."

"Strong, you mean."

"Yes. And that makes things a little strained between us, for a while. As we both get used to the change."

Bonnie was quiet. Then she made a humphing sound. "You used to be so sweet." She grinned suddenly, the fine wrinkles in her round face deepening. Frannie was struck again with why she loved her bossy aunt so much when Bonnie added with charming frankness, "You used to be so delightfully easy to order around."

"Exactly. And when I married Kenneth, and *he* started ordering me around, you and I hardly saw each other—since the two of you never got along."

"But now, since you're becoming so strong," Bonnie concluded, her head tipped to the side, "no matter who you get involved with, he won't be able to keep you from visiting your dear old Aunt Bonnie. Is that what you're telling me?"

"Exactly."

"So I am expected to be grateful that you never do what you're told anymore?"

Frannie laughed. "Yes."

"Well," Bonnie conceded, "I *am* grateful to have you near again, dear."

Frannie squeezed her aunt's plump, calloused hand. "Me, too."

Bonnie's expression grew reproving once more as she pulled her hand from Frannie's warm clasp. "But I still don't like it. A man you don't even know—"

"Aunt Bonnie. Ned St. Charles is okay. There's nothing to worry about. He's locked out of the house, and he's too drunk to make trouble, anyway."

"But Frances . . . why?" Bonnie showed her bewilderment at last.

Frannie glanced away. The question made her nervous. "He needed help," she said after a weighted moment. "And it's Christmas, after all." She knew that neither of those answers was the real one, but she just wasn't ready yet to examine her own motivations more thoroughly—or to reveal them to her disapproving Aunt Bonnie when she did.

"I don't like it," Bonnie said.

"You've made that very clear."

"He will leave tomorrow?"

"Yes, that's what I said."

"Frances, you are wearing an evasive expression."

"Because there's nothing more to say."

"You have become stubborn about *everything* lately."

"This is my house, Aunt Bonnie. I can invite anyone I like to stay in it."

"It's foolish."

"You've said that."

Bonnie sighed, and Frannie realized that her relentless aunt had at last run out of new lines of attack.

"You absolutely refuse to listen to reason?" Bonnie asked sourly.

"He's staying," Frannie replied.

Bonnie shook her head. "What in the world ever happened to my sweet little girl?"

"She finally had to grow up."

The fire popped in the stove as the two women looked at each other.

"Now you listen here," Bonnie instructed at last. "If that man gives you a bit of trouble, you just tell him I live with a sumo wrestler and that I keep an arsenal in the front hall."

"I promise," Frannie chuckled, not so much at her aunt's attempt at humor as with relief that Bonnie was finally allowing Frannie to make her own decision about this. "I'll tell him."

"Good enough." Bonnie drained the last of her cider and stood up. "It's getting late." She slid her chair back beneath the table before she went to the door. "I saw the tree in the front window. It looks beautiful."

Frannie grinned. "Wait till I get some bulbs on it."

"Whether we get along as we once did or not, I do enjoy it when you're here, Frances."

"So do I." Frannie opened the door. Both women shivered, and Bonnie stepped out onto the side porch.

"I mean it," Bonnie said. "You warn him."

"I will." Frannie watched Bonnie's retreating back as her aunt stepped off of the side porch and approached the gate between the two houses.

When she retreated back inside, Frannie glanced at the clock and thought about dinner. But she wasn't really hungry. She'd fix a sandwich later.

In the front room, her tree was waiting. She might as well get back to it.

But perhaps she should check on Ned first, make sure the electric heater was warming things up properly and see that he was covered up. He was probably very vulnerable to a chill in his condition. She'd just go down there and—

Frannie caught herself before her hand turned the lock.

The man had been down there for less than half an hour. It was not likely that much could have occurred in that amount of time. The space heater was working fine, and if he'd kicked off his blankets, he would only be likely to do it again should she tuck them around him now.

She simply had to get her mind off Ned St. Charles and back on her own activities.

Resolutely, Frannie marched through the wide door to the dining room and through that to the front parlor. She turned the Christmas record over on her old portable turntable and dug into her box of decorations with a vengeance.

In another hour, when the night outside was pitch-black save for the shimmering patterns the whirling snow made in the glow of streetlamp and porchlight, the tree was finished. Frannie climbed her stepladder to balance the star on top and then climbed down and stood back to admire what she had done.

The tree was a silver-tip fir, majestic and symmetrical, its branches rising in flat, perfect tiers. Rather than peeking out, as they would in bushier trees, the bright bulbs and holiday figurines hung between the branches, sometimes spinning with slight movements in the air, twinkling in the light.

"Nothing like a silver-tip," her dad used to say. "A silver-tip's the queen of Christmas trees. Any other tree's just a substitute in my book."

Frannie looked up, tipping her head to study the star, to see that it didn't tilt as it presided over the splendor below.

It was a homemade star, created by Frannie's own hands the Christmas she was nine. She'd shaped it from a wire hanger and wrapped it with a silver garland.

Frannie's dad had said the star was beautiful. "It's beautiful, sweetheart. You've done a fine job." He'd set the star on top of the tree with great ceremony, making sure it was placed just so, and he swore it would be their star for all the years to come.

But, of course, it hadn't been. Because that was the last year they had together. The next Christmas he was gone.

Over a decade later, she'd brought the star out again. That was during the one time she'd dragged Kenneth up here, the first year they were married. Then he was still infatuated enough with his young bride that he occasionally did things to please her.

Frannie had lifted the star out of the box, bent the crooked wires back into reasonable shape and held it up to the light, grinning proudly.

"Oh please, Frances," Kenneth had said. His handsome, distinguished face had worn no expression. His tone had been utterly flat.

There was no need to say more. The three words had said it all: the star was tacky, crudely fashioned by a child. Not the kind of thing one displayed on top of a tree. So far from perfect that it was beneath recognition.

Frannie had put it away quickly, her face flaming.

Now, a decade later, Frannie felt her face flushing all over again at the memory. But this time the flush wasn't from embarrassment. The flush was from anger.

What a cold bastard Kenneth was. But worse than that, what a weak-kneed little yes-girl she had once been. So easy to order around, just as Aunt Bonnie had said.

"But not anymore," she whispered under her breath. "Never, ever again will any man dominate me."

And she saw, in her mind's eye, the man in the basement. She saw him first as he'd been outside, when he'd begged her to take him home with her.

"Please," he'd said. And something had happened inside her, a melting kind of feeling— Kenneth had never said please. The next minute she'd heard herself offering poor, helpless Ned the basement room for the night.

Frannie closed her eyes, as if blocking out the sight of the crude star would stop the next image that came unbidden to her mind. But shutting her eyes did no good.

Against the velvet darkness of her inner eyelids, she saw Ned St. Charles as he'd been just before she left him, passed out beneath the old comforter in the bed that was too short for him.

He'd had an arm flung over his eyes, as if the slightest bit of light caused him pain. He'd groaned and then sighed. And she'd known he was asleep.

His body lay slack. Right then, for all his size and strength, he'd been completely helpless, felled by his own excesses, at the mercy of the woman who'd allowed him shelter for the night.

Frannie had stood there, rooted to the spot, and looked at the shape of his raised arm—beneath the soft, old shirt, the bulge of his bicep was clearly defined.

She'd thought how hard and strong that arm looked, how physically powerful, like the strength in his big thighs beneath the frayed overalls when she'd raised his legs onto the bed.

She had wondered, then, what it would be like to make love with a man like Ned. A simple man, with simple desires.

The idea had excited her—a hot, pulsing kind of excitement. The kind of excitement the more candid women in her support group sometimes talked about, the kind of excitement Frannie herself had never really known. Until that moment.

She had run from it. Whirled and fled up the stairs and bolted the door.

A few minutes later she'd told her aunt that Ned St. Charles represented no danger at all.

And he didn't. Ned St. Charles, of himself, was no threat to Frannie Lawry at all. She didn't need to be careful of him. The person she needed to watch like a hawk was herself.

Frannie opened her eyes and stared blankly at her tree and her wire-hanger star.

Of course, she hadn't actually fallen for Ned in the brief moments she'd spent with him. She'd only been dangerously attracted, that was all.

Frannie slumped to the sofa and leaned back on the pillows, still gazing at the star she had made as a child.

No, she hadn't fallen for him. Yet. And the *yet* was the problem.

Ned St. Charles absolutely had to go. In the morning, without fail.

Chapter Four

"Mr. St. Charles?"

Hating to do it, Burnett opened one eye. The diffused light from beyond the drawn shade sliced into his brain. He perceived that a tall woman with a lot of brown hair was bending over him. That was all he could take. Before the light could finish him off, he shut the eye he'd opened. "God. Go away." He rolled onto his side and yanked the comforter over his head.

She shook him. "It's morning. You have to get up."

He would have laughed at such a suggestion—but every cell in his body was screaming in hung-over agony. To laugh right now was something from which he doubted he'd ever recover.

"Mr. St. Charles. Please."

She yanked on the comforter. He held onto it, though even his fingers were in pain. "Have mercy. Get lost," he managed to croak.

But the woman, whoever she was, had no pity. She kept pulling the comforter. "It's morning," she said again, as if he hadn't become excruciatingly aware of that fact when he made the mistake of opening that eye a moment ago. "And you have to go." Cruelly, she ripped the comforter away. He groaned and brought up his hands to shield his hapless eyes. She grasped his shoulder—to turn him faceup again, he assumed.

But then he forgot everything as his stomach seemed to rise, inexorably, toward his throat.

"Oh, God." He surged toward the edge of the bed, knowing everything was coming up way before he could get his aching body to go anywhere.

She must have understood what was happening, because suddenly she had a big bowl in her hand and was guiding him over it.

He was sick, repeatedly. Thanks to the merciless woman, though, it was mostly in the bowl.

When he was done, he flopped on his back and wished he was dead.

"Is that all?" the woman asked.

"Isn't that enough?" he somehow got out in response.

He was nebulously aware that she left—probably to empty the bowl. But he didn't waste a lot of time thinking about the woman. He mostly cursed his own self-indulgent idiocy and lived through the agony that being in his body right then represented.

His whole self was raw, just raw. Every muscle seemed to spasm and quiver. He imagined that criminals flayed alive in the Middle Ages probably hadn't felt this bad; at least they hadn't been skinned *inside,* which was what he felt like after losing the contents of his stomach—as if most of his internal organs had come up with yesterday's Scotch.

He was distracted from the gruesome contemplation of his own pain by the sound of the door opening. The woman spoke again. "Now just what am I going to do with you?"

Burnett groaned.

"We had an agreement that you would leave in the morning," she said. "But I suppose now you'll say you don't remember it."

"Could you please stop talking?" he whispered.

"What?"

"The sound of talking hurts."

She fell blessedly silent, but not for long.

She said, "All right. I'll be back to check on you in a couple of hours. We'll try to get some liquids in you then."

He said nothing. The ability to speak had left him, or so it seemed. He breathed, slowly, trying to slip the oxygen in without letting his body know. His body didn't want to move; even the slight expansion and contraction of breathing was too much for it. At some point a little later, he gratefully lost consciousness once more.

"All right. Let's try a few spoonfuls of this broth." She was back.

"You said a coupl'a hours," he made himself complain in that hoarse croak that was all he had for a voice right then.

"It's after nine," she said, as if that explained anything.

"Do you...have to answer so fast?" he grumbled. Then, "Oh, God" again, as she shoved her hands under his arms and began pushing him upright. "Oh, please..." He felt the wall at his back. He was sitting. He kept his eyes tightly closed, thinking that right then the pain was just bearable, but if he let the light in through his eyes, the pain would be too much. "Whoever you are, I hate you," he said.

She chuckled.

"A man is dying—and you laugh," he nobly accused. "And I refuse to open my eyes."

"Fine. Just open your mouth. I'll spoon it in."

"What?"

"I told you. Beef broth."

He smelled it then. His stomach began to rise. "I can't..." he warned.

"You can. And you will. Open your mouth."

She sounded so sure that his stomach wouldn't dare make trouble again, that he did as she said. In went a spoonful of broth. He dared to swallow, then held his breath.

"It's staying down," he ventured after a nervous count of ten.

"Good. Open again."

She patiently ladled several spoonfuls into his mouth, waiting each time until he swallowed before dipping up another. Once, while she fed him, he opened his eyes. He saw pale skin and wild hair, and decided that he had been right before. The pain of the light was simply too much at this point. For the rest of the time that she fed him, he kept his eyes closed. He felt her hand brush the side of his face once; it was a cool hand, and slightly rough. He wondered what she did with her hands that made them rough. But he didn't wonder long. Wondering, like thinking in general, just caused his head to pound.

"Okay, good," she said finally. He heard her set the soup bowl down. Then she pushed on his shoulders, guiding him back flat.

He sighed. He still felt like hell, but he no longer wished he was dead.

"Who are you?" he asked.

"We covered that yesterday."

"A name, that's all," he complained. "I'd like to know what to call you while you torture me."

"Think about it," she said flatly. "It'll come to you."

He tried to remember, though it caused his brain considerable pain. He thought of a red jacket, of strange blue eyes. "Frannie," he muttered. "Frannie." He actually felt himself smile. "Right?"

"Right." Her voice was distant.

He opened his eyes again, and actually looked directly at her for the first time that morning. She was not smiling back.

"What's the matter?" he asked, a little bewildered. Though the recollection was fuzzy, he remembered she'd been sweet and good and kind yesterday. She'd patiently assisted him across the road to her house, where she'd helped him off with his jacket and boots and gently tucked him into this lumpy little bed.

He'd imagined her an angel, he recalled now. *His* angel, sent to save him from the empty wasteland that had become his life.

Right now she didn't look too angelic. She was glaring at him like a female drill sergeant with a rebellious recruit.

"Nothing's the matter," she said coldly. Her strange eyes were as expressionless as her voice. "Sleep some more. I'll be back down at noon. You'll get some solid food in you. Then you are out of here. Understand?"

Burnett frowned. Even flat on his back, nobody talked to him like that. "I'll leave now," he said, and sat up. Hot needles pierced his brain. "Sweet Lord..." he groaned, and closed his eyes.

"Down." She shoved him flat, surprising him with her strength. "You couldn't walk if you tried, and it's still snowing out. Noon will be soon enough. Sleep." Before he could tell her that he thought she was a bitch, she left.

He lay there and practiced opening and closing his eyes for a while, rather pleased that he could do that now without feeling as if a cruel hand had just shoved a burning stick into his head. And then, though he didn't plan to, he went to sleep again.

He woke the next time on his own, feeling impatient. It took him a few minutes to realize the feeling was physical; he needed to relieve himself. Bad.

He sat up, though his head protested, and threw back the comforter. He swung his legs to the floor and grimaced at his stockinged feet. He shot a glance at the battered boots he'd been wearing, then groaned. Lace-up boots. No way. His need was way beyond fumbling with lace-up boots.

He stood up, his head pounding and his stomach pitching. But when he got on his feet, he stayed there. He pulled open the door to a wall of frigid air, and confronted the basement.

In his mind, he replayed the grueling walk across the concrete floor the evening before and decided it was unlikely there might be a bathroom down here. He glanced up the stairs and saw the door that must lead to the main house.

He thought of his angel, who'd become a real harpy in the harsh light of day. Hadn't she warned him last evening that she was going to dead-bolt that door? Now, if he pounded on it, she probably wouldn't answer. She'd wait, smirking, until he disgraced himself in his overalls and then she'd come flouncing down here crowing *I told you so,* and order him out into the snow.

"No thank you," he growled aloud, and faced the opposite wall and the rough wooden door that led outside.

Outside, he concluded, was going to have to do. He stepped down to the concrete.

Even through his thick socks, it was like walking on a slab of ice. He made it quickly to the wooden door, and yanked on it.

Thank God, it was open. She hadn't gone down there and padlocked it from the outside just to torture him further, after all.

Squinting his poor, abused eyes against the glare of daylight on new snow, he stepped out of the basement and onto more, even colder concrete, beneath the overhang of the side porch.

He heard a continuous roar, and wondered what it was for a moment. Then it came to him. He was less than a hundred yards from the levee that held back the Yuba River.

All that water. Flowing.

The thought made him groan. He quickly took care of his problem, and the relief was a wonderful thing.

He stood there for a few minutes afterward, staring toward the levee, registering the fact that the snow had finally stopped, the sun was out, and he would soon, the good Lord willing, feel like a human being again.

From over on Main Street, he heard a loud, long siren go off. He had no way of knowing that the siren sounded every day at noon, or that behind him, in the basement, Frannie was just reaching the foot of the stairs.

Seconds later, Frannie stood before the entrance to the little room. She stared at the open door and saw that Ned St. Charles wasn't in there.

She glanced down to the other end of the concrete floor and saw that the outside door was open. For a moment Frannie was sure that Ned St. Charles was gone.

She didn't move. She felt . . . what? A sort of sinking feeling, a gray feeling, as if all the color had gone out of the day.

But then she glanced into the room again and spied his boots and coat. He must have only gone outside for a moment, she reasoned. Before she could stop it, a pleased smile was curving her lips. Her heart picked up a faster rhythm.

Frannie shook herself, and ordered herself to stop behaving like a lovesick fool. She'd come down here to get him up and make him eat. After that, she was going to give him a few dollars and send him out of her life once and for all.

Shivering, Frannie stepped into the little room and shut the door to seal out the cold. She went to the electric heater and let it blast some hot air around her ankles, feeling absurdly anxious and on edge. Her glance, as agitated as the rest of her, flickered around the tiny room as if there might be something new to look at there.

She noticed again the dingy jacket, which was draped over the lone straight chair in the corner. And she recalled that yesterday afternoon, out on the levee, he had put something from his wallet back into the jacket pocket. She wondered now—what could it have been?

It was none of her business. She knew it. But after the attraction she'd felt toward him last night, after the silly, impossible feelings she was having right now, she longed for any proof that showed her aunt's opinion of him to be the right one.

She longed to find out he'd lied to her, that he wasn't really Ned St. Charles at all, but some rat up to no good, who'd given her a false name and taken advantage of her sympathy for him.

If he'd lied to her, it would be easier to keep on being cold to him, easier not to smile back if he smiled at
her, easier to tell herself she had the problem of his
questionable fascination for her thoroughly under
control.

Frannie tiptoed across the room, swift and silent,
and scooped up the jacket, hardly pausing to think that
it wouldn't take much time at all for a man to take care
of his business in the snow.

Out behind the house, Burnett was enjoying his first
positive thoughts in days. He found himself thinking
that maybe getting so plastered he hardly knew his own
name hadn't been such a big mistake after all. Now that
the hangover was receding a little, and the natural
health of his big body was reasserting itself, he could
feel rather grateful just to be alive.

His divorce from Amanda was final, and actually,
that was a good thing. Even yesterday, when he'd felt
so damned despondent, he hadn't regretted the ending
of their so-called marriage. No, his depression had
been more about his failure to find love and happiness, when everything else seemed to be going so well.

He owned and operated twelve ice-cream stores that
his family had started back when he was eleven.
Sometime after the first of the year, he would be signing on twelve new franchises, which would double his
holdings. He was well-to-do now. By next Christmas,
he would be rich.

And yet it all felt kind of hollow at the core. That's
why the realization that his marriage was at last truly
and finally over had hit him so hard; in the family, he'd

always thought of himself as the stable one, the responsible one. And yet here he was, divorced with no children. Thirty-eight, with no one to call his own.

Burnett shook his head, and turned away from the hard glitter of the new snow. Better not to start dwelling on it all again. Better to take this new day and make the most of it, whatever it might bring. He'd get his angel-turned-drill sergeant to lend him her phone. He'd call the office, and have some money wired to him right away.

He realized that his feet were freezing as he ducked into the basement once more. He took the concrete floor in six big steps, in a hurry now, flush with the intention to get back to his life—lacking in real meaning as it might be—in Sacramento.

Tomorrow was Christmas Eve. He'd spend it and Christmas Day with his mother and brother and his brother's family. And he'd be grateful for all of them, that they had continued to care for him in spite of all he'd put them through over the years.

He remembered, just as he reached the closed door to the small room, about the old Jeep parked on the street across the bridge, opposite the St. Charles Place bar. Chances were, he didn't even need to wire for money, he realized. Given half a tank of gas, he could make it the hundred miles to Sacramento, and worry about money when he got home.

He pushed open the door, not remembering that he had left it ajar behind him until he heard the gasp of the woman who'd tortured him all morning. She whirled to face him, clutching his jacket in her hands.

"Oh!" she said, her wild hair flying out, her pale skin flooding with guilty color. It didn't take a brain surgeon to figure out that she'd been just about to go through his pockets.

"Looking for anything in particular?" he inquired.

Frannie stared back at him, her heart racing in her chest, all too aware that her face wore an obvious hand-in-the-cookie-jar expression. Worst of all, she hadn't explored his pockets yet, so she wasn't going to find out what he'd stuck in there yesterday.

"I...well..." she stammered, sounding just as culpable as she knew she looked.

"Yes?" he asked on a pointedly rising inflection.

Nothing to do, she decided, but brazen it out. She smoothed the ragged coat and laid it neatly back on the straight chair. "Well...there you are finally," she said, doing her best to drum up a little disapproval of him for leaving the room, in order to take the pressure off of herself for rifling his clothes. "It's time for lunch."

He folded his arms over his broad chest and studied her for a moment, a knowing smirk on his lips. Then he shrugged, apparently deciding not to challenge her further about snooping.

"Lunch?" he asked.

"Yes. It's ready now."

"Am I to be allowed inside the house for this event?" he quizzed with heavy irony.

She belligerently scowled at him. "Do you think you can behave yourself?"

"I will sincerely try, ma'am." He didn't sound sincere at all, but she decided to let it pass. To get him fed and out of her house, that was the goal.

"Put on your boots and come upstairs, then," she instructed, and then boldly took the few steps to where he stood blocking the door. "Excuse me," she said, keeping her head high.

"Certainly, ma'am," he told her, stepping to the side. She marched right past him and up the stairs, very careful with every step not to falter or look back.

Chapter Five

Burnett dipped up a spoonful of the hot, brothy vegetable soup and brought it to his lips. It was damn good. He told the silent woman across the table from him as much.

"Thank you." She delicately sipped from her own spoon, and then looked out the window at the pine-covered mountains across the river.

He shrugged, and spread creamy butter on the hot rolls she'd provided. Then he silently ate, drinking the cold milk with as much determination as he devoured the soup and rolls.

After the first few shaky bites, the food went down fine, and he was glad for it. The queasiness was passing. He felt better almost by the minute now.

What he could use, he thought, was a good workout. That would clear out the lingering fuzziness in his head, banish the faint sour taste in his mouth, burn off the shakiness from his legs and arms.

He grunted. Time enough for that when he reached home. There, he'd retreat to his private gym in the back of the house and jump rope until the last cobwebs in his brain had been completely swept away.

"More?" the woman, Frannie, was asking.

"Thank you, I'd like that," he said.

She ladled him up another helping from the big white tureen between them. He ate some more, aware that across the table she had finished eating and was watching him.

He glanced up. Her gaze slid away to the mountains again. He studied the fine line of her jaw and the pink perfection of her mouth in profile. He also noted that sometime before they sat down, probably while he was washing his face and hands, she'd pulled back her unruly hair and anchored it at her neck with a big tortoiseshell clip.

Still studying the western hills, she reached up a slim, short-nailed hand to smooth her hair. He recognized the action as a nervous one; she had felt his gaze on her hair. He watched her hand, and remembered the touch of it on his skin earlier—cool and slightly rough.

He wondered again what she did that made her hands rough—and it no longer made his head pound to ponder that. He realized he wanted to know more about her, but wasn't sure how to go about finding out. He'd never been good with casual conversation.

Since he was big and reasonably good-looking, Burnett knew most women—and men, too—perceived him as purposely remote. That had always been fine with him. Much better, he thought, than that they should know the truth; that he was shy and socially inexperienced.

He'd been the man of his family since the day his father headed off for a little fun in Lake Tahoe—and never came back. Burnett had been eleven. He'd gone to work behind the counter of the ice-cream store his mother bought, determined to do everything in his power to see that his family survived and prospered. Maybe he'd carried his dedication to duty a bit far. He'd had little time to make friends—and no time at all for girls.

He'd met Amanda when he bought his house off of Fair Oaks Boulevard. She'd been the real estate agent—and she'd taken one look at his financial statement and decided that here was the man for her. She'd pursued him relentlessly, always somehow making it seem as if he were the one chasing her. That had been fine with him, Burnett realized now. He'd felt masculine and commanding. He'd never had to confront his own shyness as long as Amanda was around. She'd hung on his arm and looked up at him adoringly and told him he was wonderful. The day they were married, he'd thought he had everything.

Remembering his own foolishness, Burnett chuckled aloud.

"What's so funny?" Frannie snapped, looking at him directly for once and narrowing her eyes.

"Nothing." He glanced at the fat, black stove in the corner, and decided to try breaking the ice by asking her something truly harmless. "You use only wood heat here?"

She looked at him, just a glance, as if checking to see if he was up to no good. Then she answered, grudgingly, "There is gas heat throughout the house, but yes, I mostly use wood."

"Wood can be expensive."

"My dad was born here and I have several distant relatives in town. Someone's always clearing trees off their property. I get wood for free, or nearly so—and I don't actually live up here anyway." She fell silent, and her mouth grew tight, as if she thought she'd revealed too much.

"Where *do* you live?"

"Why?" The word was suspicion personified.

"Just making conversation." He grinned, absurdly proud of himself because he was doing just that.

She looked even more suspicious at his grin, but allowed, "I live in Sacramento."

He started to say he lived there, too. But then he remembered that he'd given her some wild story about being from Graeagle the night before. Maybe it would be better, since he'd be leaving in a little while anyway, to just let her go on thinking that what he'd told her of himself last evening was the truth.

But then a thought struck him. Out on the levee, he'd been proud as only a drunk can be of having the foresight to salvage his driver's license before he threw his wallet in the Yuba. He'd stuck the license in the pocket of his old coat.

A little while ago he'd caught her with that coat in her hands. If she'd seen the license, then she might already know where he lived—as well as that he'd lied to her about who he was.

Burnett stared out the window himself for a moment, wondering if he owed her some kind of explanation, and not really feeling up to providing one. When he returned home, he'd send her a check for her trouble, along with a little note explaining why he'd pretended to be Ned St. Charles. In the note, he'd remind her how drunk he'd been, and point out that his reasoning had been completely skewed.

You're not drunk now, a chastening voice in his head suggested.

So?

So, the responsible thing to do would be to tell the truth before you leave here...

"Ned?" she asked softly from across the table, putting an end to his internal dialogue. He looked at her, registering the lack of irony in her use of the name, and deciding she must not have seen the license after all. She still believed he was who he'd said he was. He felt relief, but refused to examine the feeling.

He looked at her, raising a brow. "Yes?"

She swallowed, and her eyes slid away once more. "Nothing. I don't know." Her voice was soft. He realized that the icy facade she'd maintained between them had melted away sometime during his extended silence. She pushed her empty soup bowl away a little and folded her hands on the table. "You seemed far away," she said. "And tense, just then." He could see that she was concerned for him, worried perhaps that his being quiet for so long might mean something grave. "You're going to be all right, aren't you?"

"I'll be fine," he said.

"Good. I'm glad," she said. Then she smoothed her hair again and stood up. "Finished?" She gave him a forced, bright smile, which he saw as an attempt to reclaim some of the distance between them, distance that had dangerously dissolved in the past few minutes.

He nodded. "Thank you," he said, picking up her formal tone. "It was delicious."

She began gathering the bowls and spoons. He rose and helped her, carrying the remaining rolls to the counter, and after that the big white tureen.

When he set the tureen down beside her, she turned to reach for the sponge. Her arm brushed his.

It was nothing, really. Hardly enough even to be called a touch. But his breath caught, briefly, in his throat at the warmth that radiated from her. He was inordinately aware of the way she stiffened and pulled back.

"Excuse me," she said, as if she'd done something impolite.

"No problem," he responded, his own face reddening at how utterly inane that sounded.

They both cleared their throats then, and she busily began wiping down the counters, while he stood back, stuck his hands into his pockets and tried not to stare at her skin and her hair and the way her lashes brushed her cheeks whenever she lowered her eyes.

When at last the evidence of the lunch had been cleaned away, she asked him with diffident courtesy, "Won't you sit down again, Ned?" She smiled, fleetingly, as their eyes met.

The slight flush that came to her cheeks before she glanced away told him that he hadn't imagined her reaction to their quick, brushing touch. She was attracted to him—or at least, to Ned—even if she didn't want to be.

As he took his chair, she disappeared through the door to the dining room. She returned in no time at all and sat down herself. Then she cleared her throat, the way people do when sneaking up on a delicate subject.

She looked at him through those incredible eyes— how could he have forgotten, even while she was torturing him earlier, what unbelievable eyes she had?

And had she really been so rough on him? Of course not. She'd done what she had to do with him to help him get sober.

And now he *was* sober, thanks mostly to her. And he could look at her beautiful face and hear her soft voice and completely comprehend why he had thought her his angel the evening before.

"Ned?" she said hesitantly.

"Yes?"

"I want you to take this money." She pushed a few bills across the table at him. "I know you need it."

He looked at the bills for a moment, and then pushed them back to her. "I can't take that," he said, just as he imagined Ned might. With proud restraint. A good, responsible man fallen on hard times, who was still above charity.

"It's okay, really. You can pay me back," she said, sounding strained.

He put his hands in his lap and looked down at the beat-up surface of the table. He knew what was coming next. She was getting ready to ask him to leave.

And he just wasn't ready to leave quite yet. Suddenly his life in Sacramento was seeming empty again. While here, in this big, old-fashioned kitchen, there was warmth and nourishment and a pretty woman who blushed when her eyes met his.

But how was he going to convince her to let him stay for a while?

An idea occurred to him immediately, and he put it to use without even stopping to think; he decided to do what he imagined Ned would do—go on the offensive, because of injured pride.

He looked up, setting his face in defiant lines. "What do you mean, I can pay you back?" he demanded, and watched as she gasped, surprised at his sudden wounded vehemence. "You don't ever expect to see a penny of this money again. It's charity, pure and simple. And I don't want it. Understand?"

She looked stricken. "I didn't mean to insult you," she said. "I only thought..."

"What?" he demanded. "What did you think?" Her gaze slid away. "And stop looking out the window. Look at me."

She straightened up and faced him. "All right. I thought you could use a few dollars to get you back to Graeagle. If you won't take the money, that's your business. But now I want you to go."

"Why?"

The word hung between them for a moment. Then she said, "It was what we agreed."

"I was drunk," he said.

She glared at him. "It was a perfectly reasonable agreement, no matter what state you were in. This is my house and you are taking advantage of my hospitality—for as long as I choose to extend it. And I told you from the first that you were only here until morning. Well, morning has come and gone. Your welcome is worn out."

He looked at her flushed face and guarded expression, thinking that, while her argument was completely acceptable, there was much more to her urgency that he be gone than what she was telling him.

She felt the same attraction he felt, he was sure of it—and she didn't like it one bit. He couldn't fault her for that; she was displaying nothing less than sound judgment. To her, he was a down-and-out drunk she'd pulled out of the snow. Pursuing an attraction to him would be foolhardy.

He understood that he should say *thank you for all you've done* and get up and go. But he didn't. Some perverse part of him wanted her to admit the *real* reason she was so anxious to see him leave.

He prodded, "You still haven't answered my question."

"What question?"

"Why you are so anxious to see the last of me?"

She squinted at him as if he weren't very bright. "Didn't I just explain that?"

"You said I'd worn my welcome out."

"And you have."

"Because I was drunk and disorderly and you've been having to play nursemaid all morning?"

"Yes. That's right."

"And that's all?"

"What are you getting at?"

"Is it? All?"

"It's enough, I should say."

"But it isn't everything."

She was quiet for a moment. Then, "I don't choose to go into this any further." She stood up. "Take the money, Ned. Send me a check general delivery, care of Bonnie Lawry when you have it."

"No," he said.

Her face was cold and set again, her voice hard. "All right. That's up to you. But I do want you to leave now."

He stood up, slowly, and they faced each other across the table. Her strange eyes commanded—yet seemed to plead at the same time.

Burnett began to feel like a heel. She'd been nothing but generous to him, and here he was baiting her to confess an attraction that all wisdom demanded she should deny.

"I want you to leave," she said again, her gaze locked with his. He said nothing. He was thinking how beautiful and vulnerable she looked. He was wondering what she would do if he reached across the table and—

"Don't..." It was a plea, as if she'd read his thoughts in his eyes.

He didn't move.

"You must leave." Now she truly sounded desperate.

"Please..." he said, thinking vaguely that, since he'd met her, he'd been using that word as if he said it all the time.

"Ned, I mean it . . ."

"What?"

"You can't stay here."

"I know," he said, though he didn't know. Not at all. "But I'd just like to . . ."

"Yes?"

"There's one more thing I'd like to say."

"All right."

"Don't answer too fast, okay?" he urged. "Give it just a little thought."

She promised she would.

He began hesitantly, "You pulled me out of the snow, put me up for the night. Then you nursed me this morning. I've caused you nothing but trouble. At least let me do a little something for you around here. To work off what I owe you."

"Ned, I . . ."

"Please."

She started to shake her head, and then stopped at the sound of a sharp knock that came from behind him. Burnett turned his head. Through the glass at the top of the side door, he saw a gray-haired woman with a round face, a prim mouth and a downright antagonistic expression.

"It's Aunt Bonnie," Frannie said, then louder, "Come on in."

The stocky little woman bustled in the door. "I made some fudge." She held out a plate veiled in plastic wrap. "I knew you'd want some, dear."

"Thanks," Frannie said, dryly, as if she were well aware that her aunt had more than fudge on her mind.

"I'll just set it right here on the counter," the little woman went on.

"Great."

"And then, I can only stay for one cup of coffee."

"There's some in the coffeemaker." Frannie's voice was resigned.

"Well, I know that. I can see. And I'll just help myself." Aunt Bonnie did precisely that, scurrying to the coffeepot and then to the head of the table between Burnett and Frannie. Frannie sighed and sat back down. Burnett, wary of the way the woman's small dark eyes bored through him, but glad of the reprieve from being told again to leave, followed suit.

"Well now," Aunt Bonnie said pointedly as soon as they were all three settled in their chairs. "This must be the man you pulled out of the snow last evening, Frances." She looked from Frannie to Burnett and then back again. "He looks well enough now."

"Aunt Bonnie, this is Ned St. Charles," Frannie said, her voice studiously bland. "Ned, Bonnie Lawry."

Burnett held out his hand. "Pleased to meet you, Mrs. Lawry," he said with a slight drawl that surprised him a little coming out of his mouth. Burnett Clinton never drew out his words. But somehow, he was realizing, Ned St. Charles did.

Bonnie Lawry looked at his hand a long time before taking it. "It's *Miss*," she said at last, condescending to shake. The she looked down at the hand that engulfed hers. She looked up again, her expression more distrustful than ever. Right then, Burnett was sure that Aunt Bonnie had noticed what her niece hadn't: his

hands were smooth, the nails trimmed. Hands like his
didn't belong on a man who couldn't even afford a
motel room for the night.

Bonnie began tartly, "I hear you're from Graeagle,
Mr. St. Charles." She put just the slightest emphasis on
the name St. Charles, and Burnett was sure that it was
her way of telling him she knew very well what the bar
on Main Street was called.

"Yes," he said, dreading whatever she would ask
next. "I drove over from Graeagle yesterday, that's
right."

"Not a lot of work in Graeagle," she remarked.
"Especially in the winter, when all the tourists go
home."

"That's true," he said noncommittally, "it's mostly
a tourist town, from what I hear."

"From what you hear? I thought you lived there."

"Aunt Bonnie, that's enough," Frannie said, her
face pinkening.

"It's all right," Burnett said, loathing the quizzing
aunt, but keeping sight of his objective: to get Frannie
to allow him to stay. He wasn't going to get what he
wanted by being surly to her relatives. He smiled at
Bonnie. "No, ma'am, I don't live there. I've just been
staying there for a couple of days."

Burnett was aware of Frannie across the table, of her
tense regard. The aunt's questions, he realized, were
probably ones she herself had wanted to ask, but
hadn't quite managed. The attraction between them
had kept her too wary and nervous around him to pry.

Bonnie, however, had no such problem. She wanted
to know about this Ned St. Charles, and she had no

compunction about coming right out and accusing, "You told my niece that you were from Graeagle."

"He was drunk, Aunt Bonnie," Frannie answered before he could. "And it was true. He'd come from Graeagle, and that was where he would have returned, had he been in any condition to drive." The aunt made a humphing sound. Frannie bristled, "It was a simple slipup in communication, that's all."

Burnett held back a fatuous grin. The last thing he'd expected was for Frannie to leap to his defense. Maybe he was closer to being allowed to stay than he imagined.

He glanced at Frannie. She met his eyes briefly and then looked at Bonnie once more. Burnett realized he'd lose whatever ground he'd gained if he didn't join in his own defense. He put on an abashed expression and said to the aunt, "I've been having a rough time lately. And a...friend offered me the use of his family cabin there, to kind of pull myself together."

"What friend?"

"Burnett's his name," he said, almost without thinking. It was, in a strange way, the truth. "Burnett Clinton."

"This Burnett Clinton is a *close* friend of yours?" Bonnie asked.

Burnett swallowed. "Very close. We grew up together."

"Where was that?"

"Sacramento."

"Is that where you actually live, then?"

"Yes. It is." He felt the quick flick of Frannie's glance and feared she was finding it suspicious that he hadn't mentioned he lived in Sacramento when she told him she lived there. But then, he reasoned, that had been an emotionally charged moment. He'd fallen silent. And she'd asked him if he was going to be all right. If she thought about that exchange, she could interpret it any number of ways.

"And exactly what kind of work do you do?" the relentless aunt continued.

"I'm a...manager, among other things."

"Manager of what?"

"Aunt Bonnie, you are being downright rude," Frannie said rather hotly.

Her aunt tossed her a pugnacious little scowl. "*Somebody* has to find out who this person is that you've taken under your roof."

"It's my roof, and my business," Frannie shot back, every bit as belligerent as the little woman to her right.

"Ladies..." Burnett began.

Both women glared at him. He decided to say no more, realizing that there was more going on here than he understood, some kind of conflict between the aunt and niece that had been in progress well before he landed in the snowbank out back.

"In any case," Bonnie said brusquely after a moment of heated silence, "It's past noon, and you said he would be gone in the morning."

Burnett longed to tell Aunt Bonnie exactly what he thought of women who spoke of him in the third person when he was sitting right there. But he didn't. He counted to ten, and tried to remember that he was supposed to be an unassuming guy named Ned, who probably put women on a pedestal and who was surely accustomed to having people talk about him as if he wasn't even in the room.

He was grateful he'd kept his mouth shut when he heard what Frannie said next. "Well, I changed my mind."

"You *what?*" the aunt demanded, puffing up her already considerable chest so that she resembled an enraged mother hen.

"You heard what I said," Frannie flatly announced. "There's kindling to split in the basement, and logs that need to be cut down to size. Ned's going to take care of it for me. He'll be here at least until dark, the way I see it."

"But, Frances..." Aunt Bonnie sputtered.

Longing to throw back his head and crow in triumph, Burnett stood up before Frannie could think twice and change her mind.

"And that reminds me," he murmured in the soft-spoken drawl that was beginning to seem like a natural way to talk. "I'd better get to work. Nice to meet you, Miss Lawry. And Frannie, thanks for the lunch. It was mighty fine."

A half hour later, beneath the back porch where the chopping block was, Burnett sunk the ax into the hard hunk of oak, worked it out, and then brought it down again. Once cut in two, the log would be about stove-size. With the next stroke, one half of the log fell to the concrete beside the block.

Burnett laid the ax carefully against the block, hoisted the fallen half of the log, and tossed it onto the pile he was making of stove-ready wood to stack in the basement. He tossed the other half right after it.

Then he brushed his bare hands off—they were already a little tender, and tomorrow they would have blisters. The thought gave him some satisfaction, though he wasn't sure why. Maybe he wanted to punish himself for deceiving a woman who'd only been kind to him—though he wasn't willing to do the right thing and tell her the truth. Maybe he wanted to toughen his hands a little, since the sharp-eyed aunt had seemed to notice them as too smooth for the kind of man he claimed to be.

Hell, Burnett thought. Who could say why he was out here chopping wood without gloves? Who could say why he'd done *anything* he'd done in the past twenty-four hours?

He chose another log, set it on the block. Then he hefted the ax again, bringing it down with a resounding thwack.

He worked for a while steadily and smoothly; Burnett was no stranger to chopping wood. The cabin in Graeagle was heated with wood, and both he and his brother had learned to cut logs and kindling as soon as they were old enough to lift an ax.

Though the temperature in the shade was in the thirties, sweat had started on his body beneath the old flannel shirt he wore. He was content with that. After all, he'd wanted a workout, hadn't he? His blood, which had felt sluggish in his veins after the way he'd abused himself yesterday, had started pumping hard and clean again.

The tumbled pile of stove-ready logs grew. When it was high enough to fill the holes in the neat stacks inside the basement, he found some pine and a short ax and began to cut kindling, shaving it off the logs as a chef might slice a pineapple, turning the logs, paring them down to their pale cores.

The job was somewhat mesmerizing and pleasant in the hypnotic way of work that becomes mindless once the rhythm has been established. He was almost done when he heard Frannie's voice, gently chiding, from behind him.

"You could have asked for gloves."

He smiled to himself. Here it was, another opportunity to be honest. He could tell her just what he'd been thinking a while ago, that he'd set to work glove-less for at least two possible reasons—both of them reprehensible.

He set down the short ax, turned and gave her a broad smile, wiping the sweat from his brow with the back of his hand.

She was wearing her red jacket and holding out a pair of heavy gloves. Her hair was loose and wild around her face again. He reached out and took the gloves without letting go of her gaze, thinking that the last thing he was willing to do right now was be honest. If she knew that everything about him was a lie, he'd lose what little ground he'd gained since he'd broken the ice at lunch.

Later, he thought. He would tell her all of it later. After he knew her better, after he was sure of the right way to go about explaining it.

"Thanks," he said, still lost in her eyes. "I'm almost done with the ax, but these'll help for stacking."

"You'll have blisters." He felt the light brush of her hand on his—a swift touch, quickly withdrawn. Her face pinkened enchantingly.

"Doesn't matter."

They stood in tableau for timeless seconds. On the cold winter air, he got a whiff of her scent. It was light. Fresh and floral. He stepped back, feeling suddenly awkward and earthbound, musty with sweat.

She looked away, toward the levee and the drawn-out sigh of the river beyond. "She left, finally. Aunt Bonnie, I mean." She looked back, and gave a nervous chuckle. "But not before she told me you were nothing but trouble, and I was a foolish, foolish girl." Her voice pretended to accuse him. "You certainly didn't waste any time flying down those stairs when I told her you were staying to chop wood for me."

"I've learned a few things in my life, appearances to the contrary."

"Such as?"

"In this case, when opportunity knocks, open the door and grab it, before it gets away."

She laughed, and then grew pensive. "I know hardly anything about you."

He looked at her—steadily, he hoped. "What do you want to know? All you have to do is ask."

"All right." She paused, then queried, "How long have you been out of a job, Ned?"

"I'm not," he told her, absolving himself of some of his guilt by trying to stretch the truth without actually lying.

"You do have a job?"

He nodded. "I work for that friend of mine I mentioned to your aunt."

"Oh, yes. Burnett—"

"Clinton," he supplied the last name she'd been searching for.

"What do you do?"

"Well, Burnett owns a chain of ice-cream stores, and I help him out. I do . . . odd jobs for him."

"Like?"

He shrugged, trying to look unconcerned while he frantically sought a believable list of duties to report to her. Then it occurred to him, the things a guy like Ned might do.

"Fix equipment, maintenance, things like that," he said.

Once again he'd told a half-lie. As a kid, Burnett had always loved to figure out how things worked, to fix what was broken. Until well into his teens, he'd done the repairs at his family's ice-cream stores himself.

But then he'd wanted to attend college, and after that he'd gradually taken over complete control of the business from his mother, who was more than happy to relinquish it. It had become economically unfeasible for him to spend his time fiddling with the equipment, so from then on he'd hired professionals to do that kind of work.

"You're a repairman?" she was asking.

"Partly." He remembered what he'd told her aunt. "And sometimes I run individual stores, manage them, you know, when one manager leaves before a new one hires on."

"And this friend, Burnett, gave you some time off?"

"Yeah. I've been...kind of depressed lately. And he suggested I take off until after the first of the year."

"Depressed because of your divorce, you mean?"

"Partly." He longed to change the subject, because the more he told her about himself, the more danger he would be in of contradicting himself later. "Frannie?" he asked softly.

"Yes?"

"I've wondered, since this morning..."

"What is it?"

"What do *you* do for a living?"

She grinned. "All you had to do was ask."

"Well, that's what I'm doing."

Her smile turned proud. "I'm a stagecraft teacher. At Sacramento River Junior College." At his puzzled frown, she elaborated. "I'm a drama teacher, but on the technical end. I teach scene design and stage lighting, and set construction. And I design most of the sets for productions—as well as helping to build them."

He thought of the slight roughness of her hands, and understood now how they got that way. "You like your work," he remarked in reference to her proud smile when she talked about it.

"I do," she said, and the two words held a hint of defiance. "I would never give it up."

"Has someone asked you to?"

"I was married myself once. My husband found my job an inconvenience...at best."

"Married?" he asked stupidly. It took a minute to digest that information. His angel had a life before him. He'd known that she must have, of course. But hearing her say it suddenly made it real.

"I'm thirty-three," she told him. "I haven't lived in a vacuum, you know."

"You look younger."

"I'm a grown woman." Now she seemed almost angry. "And don't you forget it."

"I won't." He tried that charming smile that Ned St. Charles seemed to do so well.

"I run my own life. No one tells me what to do."

"Hey." He raised a hand. "Truce. Please?" At last, she smiled. A slow smile, one that looked somewhat embarrassed. "I...like you, Frannie," he added then. "I'm just curious about you."

She cast her gaze toward the sky, and then looked back at him. "I understand. I get defensive about my independence. It's very important to me."

"Because you lost it once?"

She was silent, considering his question. Then she said, "Because I allowed someone to take it from me once."

"Your ex-husband?"

"Yes—and I'd prefer to change the subject now."

He put in quickly, before she could start quizzing him about himself again, "How about if I get this wood stacked in the basement?"

"Good idea." They shared another long look, and he wondered if she was thinking what he was; their second agreement—about his staying until he'd replenished her wood supply—had almost played itself out. She'd probably be insisting he leave again, when he was done. And when she did, what excuse would he find to stay this time?

He wasn't sure. But he *was* going to stay longer. Somehow. Some way. The means to that end simply hadn't occurred to him yet.

Chapter Six

"Er, excuse me..." Frannie whirled around at the sound of his voice, her heart tripping into high gear and her cheeks burning as if they'd been set on fire from within.

"Oh!" she heard herself exclaim, like a giddy, breathless schoolgirl. "You surprised me."

Actually, she'd been staring dreamily out the window above the sink at the side wall of her aunt's house. She'd been thinking of things she had no business thinking about—like the way Ned looked when he smiled, so sexy and yet sincere at the same time.

"All finished," he said.

"Finished."

"With the wood."

"Oh. Oh, yes. Of course."

"Here." He held out the work gloves. "Thanks."

She took them. "Thank *you*."

"You're welcome." He stepped back and looked down at his boots. "Listen, I..."

"Yes?" Her voice sounded ridiculously eager to her own ears.

"I was wondering—"

"What?"

"If I might..."

"What? What is it, Ned?"

"Well, I'm a mess."

She grinned at him, thinking he was right. The old shirt clung to him, wet with sweat, while the shadow of new beard darkened the bottom half of his face. At lunch, he'd scrubbed his hands and splashed some water on his face. But he needed a good, hot shower.

"I realize it's a lot to ask, after everything else you've done for me," he began, "but I wonder if I could possibly..."

Frannie hid the smile that threatened to curve her lips. He was so polite and unassuming. Except when she hurt his pride by offering him a handout, Ned had never so much as raised his voice in her presence. She was sure he came from a down-to-earth, working-class family, where he'd learned good manners and respect for authority right from the first.

In fact, the more she was around him, the more Frannie was sure that he was utterly harmless. She'd be willing to bet now that yesterday's binge had been uncharacteristic for him. He was a good man for whom things had simply been very rough lately, and he'd felt so hopeless that he'd tried to forget it all in the bottom of a bottle.

She tipped her head and studied him, not thinking that her fond thoughts would be mirrored in the softness of her eyes. "You wonder if you could possibly what?"

"Well . . . Do you think I could use your shower?"

He looked so agonized over having to ask such a thing, that Frannie was hard put to keep a straight face. "Of course you may."

Gratitude lit him up like a beacon. "Thanks."

"You're welcome." How could she have ever imagined he might be dangerous to her?

You didn't, a voice in her head reminded. It was never *him* you were worried about . . .

Frannie ignored the nagging voice of her wiser self and gestured toward the bathroom, which was just off the kitchen on the other side of the heat stove. "Help yourself. There are fresh towels on those shelves in the corner."

"Great."

"And . . . why don't you toss your clothes outside the door when you get out of them. I'll wash them, and I'm sure we can come up with something for you to put on until your own clothes are dry."

"I couldn't," he said.

"You can and you will," she told him with firm authority.

He was quiet, smiling appreciatively. And then he turned for the bathroom and his shower.

Frannie stood there for a moment, staring after him with a half smile on her face. Then she shook herself and went up the back stairs to the attic to rummage through some boxes of old clothes she knew were stored there.

What she found wasn't much of an improvement over his threadbare overalls and torn shirt, but they were reasonably clean. She returned to the kitchen to find his dirty clothes neatly folded by the bathroom door. She traded them for the ones in her arms and then went down to the basement, humming, to put his things in the washer. She paused, before remounting the stairs, to approve of the way he'd stacked the wood, ends out, packed tight and even.

And then she thought of his old jacket, just a few feet away in the little basement room. It would be such a simple thing to sneak in there now and see what it was he had kept back from the river when he threw his wallet and money away. He would never catch her at it now. He was soaking wet in the shower; she could hear the water running in the pipes. She'd be in the room and out before he could dry off and put on the clean clothes she'd provided for him.

Frannie reached for the door to the room—and then dropped her arm.

Over lunch, and in the few exchanges they'd had since then, she and Ned had almost become *friends*. One didn't go through a friend's possessions. It simply was not done.

Frannie smiled to herself and turned away from the door. Ned's secrets were his own business. She wouldn't pry into them.

When she entered the kitchen again, she noticed that the sun hung just above the mountains. Soon it would be night again. And it was time for Ned to leave.

But then the bathroom door opened, releasing a cloud of warm steam. And he emerged, wearing the clothes she'd left by the door: patched jeans that hugged his hips and another old flannel shirt—this one a solid navy blue, frayed at the collar and cuffs. His hair was wet and his face was shaved. Frannie had never seen anyone look so handsome in her entire life.

He rubbed his smooth, square jaw. "I think I completely destroyed that little pink razor of yours."

"It's all right. I have more."

"That's good."

There was another of those silences that seemed to occur all the time when he was around—those silences where they just stared at each other, smiling inanely.

"Well," he said.

"Yes?" she asked.

"I have a Jeep," he told her, as if making a confession.

"Oh."

"It's over on Main Street."

"Where on Main Street?"

"In front of the restaurant."

"Cirino's at the Forks?"

"Yeah, across from the bar." He seemed to hesitate, then continued, "The St. Charles Place bar." Did his eyes shift away? No, Frannie told herself. That his name and the name of the bar were the same was merely coincidence, that was all. Aunt Bonnie and her suspicions could go take a hike.

Ned laughed, then. And Frannie knew she was right about him when he said easily, "You know, it seemed

real meaningful to me yesterday—that I found a bar
with my name on it.''

"I'll bet,'' Frannie muttered, playfully grim.

"Don't give me that look, Frannie Lawry,'' Ned
commanded with mock severity.

"What look?''

"The disapproving look.''

"I'm not.''

"You are.''

"No.''

"Yes.''

"Uh-uh.''

"Uh-huh...''

Frannie, who could have stood there looking at him
indefinitely, didn't miss the marveling expression that
crossed his face.

"What is it?'' she asked.

"Oh, nothing...''

"Come on. Tell me.''

"It's just...''

"Yes? Please, Ned. I want to know.''

"My brother...''

She remembered last evening, he'd mentioned a
brother. "Casey, right?''

"Yes. Casey,'' he said.

"Well? What about him?''

"He's happily married.''

"Oh?''

"He married his best friend just a few years ago. A
woman we both grew up with.''

"Yes. And?''

"Just now, you and me..." His face went red. He was blushing.

Frannie thought it was wonderful to see a man do that. He looked so handsome, and...vulnerable. Something way down inside of her went very warm and soft.

"You and me what?" she prompted.

"Well..."

"Come on, you can tell me."

"I can?" He was half teasing and half serious.

"Yes. Tell me."

"We sound like them." He looked away. "That's all. It's silly."

"No," she said softly. "You don't really think it's silly, do you?"

He didn't meet her eyes, and he spoke with difficulty. "I've always envied what they had, though I used to pretend otherwise. My brother was sort of a runaround when he was younger. He had a reputation for being wild. But he always had this best friend, Joanna, who just happened to be a girl. And when they'd get together, it was always like they each knew what the other was thinking, and they'd always kind of tease each other, back and forth, like kids do, like you and me just then. And I used to almost hate them for having that, something so comfortable and *fun,* something I was sure I'd never have with anyone, let alone a girl..."

"Do you still almost hate them?" she asked when she was sure he wasn't going to go on of his own accord.

He shook his head. "We had a...family crisis, at the time the two of them were married. And since then Casey and I—and Joanna, too—have worked a lot of things out between us." He was quiet again.

Though her mind was filled with questions about his family and the family crisis and the "things" he and his brother had worked out, she didn't ask him. She felt he'd said more than he'd ever intended to and that was enough—for now.

She said, lightly, "So you've left your Jeep across from the St. Charles Place bar. And?"

He looked relieved, as if she'd rescued him from a conversational hole he'd fallen into. "And do you think it's been towed away by now?"

Frannie chuckled. "I doubt it. Around here, they give a little more leeway about things like that. Generally, they will try to find the owner of the vehicle first, and tow later. The winter population here is under four hundred. So that means we're all neighbors. And neighbors tend to want to stay on good terms with each other."

"Lucky for me."

"Yes. But, of course, you never know for sure until you go and find out."

"Yeah. And I think that's what I'd better do right now."

Outside, the sun was going. The corners of the kitchen darkened, while the light from the window cut a glaring swath through the heart of the room. Frannie, in the shadows, looked across the harsh path of light at Ned and found it hard to see his expression. He was in shadow, too.

It had been twenty-four hours, Frannie thought, since she'd pulled him from the snow. He was sober, cleaned up and ready to return to his own life. It was time for him to go.

She said, "Please let me lend you that money, Ned."

"No."

"Then take it for chopping wood."

"No." He smiled, his teeth flashing white through the shadows. "I'll get my coat." He turned and disappeared down the basement stairs, reappearing in no time at all.

"What about your clothes?" she asked as she watched him slide his arms in the old jacket.

"What about them?"

"They're still in the washer."

"They aren't important," he said quietly, after he had the jacket on. "Are these that I have on important to you?"

"No," she said. "No, they aren't important."

"Then, that's all. Isn't it?" There was a challenge in the question. He stepped out of the shadows and into the light in the center of the room. "Isn't it?"

"I suppose . . ."

He moved closer, skirting the table, until he was only a few feet from her. "You suppose what?"

That soft, liquid something was happening inside her again. She sounded like someone in a trance when she made herself tell him. "I suppose that's all."

"Over and done?" He said it very gently, so gently that she didn't even feel like backing away when she realized he had taken that one more step that put him right in front of her.

She could smell the soap on his skin, see the little nick on his jaw where her razor must have slipped once. "Ned?" She breathed, thinking of how broad his shoulders were, how deep his chest. How he was big and strong...and yet vulnerable. Someone who would never try to tell her how to run her life.

"Frannie," he whispered, smiling, as if it gave him pleasure just to say her name.

"Ned, please don't..."

"What? Don't what?"

Don't leave, she thought. "Don't do this," she said.

"What? This?" he asked as his fingers tipped her chin so lightly, just the barest of touches, enough to guide her face up to his.

"Ned?"

His lips brushed hers, once across and then back. She sighed.

And then he dropped his hand and stepped back.

"Ned?"

"Sorry," he said, looking away. Then he looked back. And he smiled. "Hell, no. I'm not. I'm not sorry at all. I've wanted to do that forever—or at least since lunch."

The kiss had been so brief, and so achingly tender, that Frannie could find no regret for it inside herself. She returned his sweet, abashed smile with a tremulous one of her own.

He said, "Your lips are soft. Just like they look." Then he chuckled. "Does that embarrass you, for me to say that?" She shook her head. "Then why are you blushing?"

"Because..."

"Yeah?"

"All right," she confessed. "It embarrasses me a little." She felt warm and wonderful... and kind of silly, too. She glanced down bashfully. He put his finger under her chin again, to coax her eyes to meet his. She reached for his hand, and he winced, ever so slightly, when she touched one of the blisters he'd acquired while chopping wood for her without gloves. They stood for a timeless moment, hand in hand, eye-to-eye.

Then, reluctantly, he pulled free of her gentle grasp and stepped back.

Their eyes still held. And then Frannie heard herself suggesting, "I'll walk with you. To your Jeep."

They turned for the side door as one, pausing briefly while Frannie put on her jacket and tucked her hair under a fleecy wool hat.

Outside, it was below freezing. Frannie quickly shoved her feet into the rubber boots that she kept on the side porch, and they walked, hands stuffed into their pockets, to the front of the house, which faced Commercial Street.

The snow lay smooth on the front yard, an unbroken blanket of white covering the lawn and the walk all the way to the low wrought-iron fence. Beyond the fence, the slate sidewalk was covered with a layer of gray snow, while the street beyond had a scraped-raw look, the work, Frannie knew, of the county snowplow.

Frannie and Ned stood on the wooden boards of the porch for a moment, and the streetlamp on the nearby Pearl Street corner came on, as if lighting their way.

They turned and grinned at each other. Then he was taking her arm and tucking it through his, and to Frannie it seemed the most natural thing in the world that he should do that.

They stepped off the porch into the foot and a half of snow together, and trudged to the front gate. At the sidewalk, they went left, down the sloping street to a bridge that crossed the Downie River, which converged with the Yuba on the west end of town. Across the bridge and down the street a ways, they came to another corner, the intersection of Commercial and Main. Both streets were adorned, all along the covered sidewalks, with live Christmas trees tied to the posts that held up the overhangs. Each tree had been decorated in a different style—some with bright bulbs and tinsel, some with paper chains, some with ornaments of cloth or straw.

Ned's battered Jeep, wearing a high cap of packed snow on the roof, waited right where he'd left it. They stopped when they reached it, and just stood there for a moment, still arm in arm.

Then Ned said, "Well. This is it."

Frannie's eyes burned suddenly. And the colored lights on the trees along the street blurred a little. But she took herself in hand. There was no way she was going to cry over a man she'd hardly known a day.

Behind her, the door to Cirino's restaurant opened, and a man and a woman who looked vaguely familiar came out. The couple nodded. Frannie said hello, and as they passed on down the street, she brusquely slid her arm from Ned's and stepped back.

"You, um, take care of yourself," she muttered awkwardly.

"Thanks. For everything," he said.

"Glad I could be of help."

"You were, more than I can say."

Then, too soon, they'd run out of all the standard phrases. He held her gaze for a moment more—and her heart jumped a little; she thought for a second that he was going to tell her he just couldn't leave, *wouldn't* leave....

But that was only the hopeless romantic inside her imagining things. He said nothing, only went around behind the Jeep to the street side and then climbed behind the wheel. He bent for a moment and groped under the seat, coming up with a key, which he inserted in the ignition.

Frannie stood on the sidewalk, bereft, her arms wrapped tightly around her body, while he fiddled with the choke and tried to get the ancient machine to turn over. At last, there was a groaning rumble, a sputter or two, and the thing was running, more or less.

There was a lump in Frannie's throat. She could hardly see for holding back the silly tears. She clutched her arms tighter around herself, as Ned, blurry through the moisture in her eyes, leaned across the seat toward her and pushed open the passenger door.

"I'll drive you back," he said over the ragged roar of the old engine.

Frannie had never jumped in a vehicle so fast in her life. She slammed the door firmly behind her. He pulled out of the space and turned around up past the community hall. They were back in front of the house her dad had left her in minutes.

He turned to her. "Here you are."

She looked at him. "I suppose you threw your driver's license in the river, too."

He shrugged.

"You could get a ticket, driving without it."

"Worse things have happened to me, believe me," he said.

She glared at him, feeling angry suddenly at what she knew she intended to say next.

She said, "All right. I've got an extra steak. Stay for dinner?"

His smile took her breath. "I thought you were never going to ask."

Chapter Seven

They ate in the dining room, which opened onto the front room. From where he sat, on the right side of the table, Burnett could see her Christmas tree in the front window. The lights on the tree were the big, old-fashioned kind, the color on the bulbs faded from years of use. Many of the ornaments looked home-made.

Frannie offered red wine with the steaks. Burnett declined even a glass. After yesterday, the thought of liquor, even of wine, made him a little queasy. But that wasn't the only reason why he refused when she tipped the bottle toward his glass. He also did it because he wanted his head clear. He did it because he had a specific goal now, and he wasn't going to allow himself to get fuzzy and mellow and put his foot in his mouth.

His goal was to stay here. At least for a few days, in this old house by the river in this charming small town. He wanted to share a white Christmas with the angel who'd dragged him from a snowbank yesterday evening. He was willing to sleep in the basement, if that was how she wanted it—though he didn't mind hoping that she might decide they could share even more than the short winter days.

Most important of all, he fully intended to tell her, before the night was over, who he really was. Because he wanted this time with her to be without lies or subterfuge.

But how exactly to go about telling her was the problem. It seemed that every time he opened his mouth to begin explaining, the words just wouldn't come out.

While he sought the proper moment to reveal all, he encouraged her to open up about herself. She told him that her dad had died when she was ten, and that her mother had remarried within a year.

"Downieville was my home," Frannie explained. "But as soon as my dad was gone, Mother moved the two of us to Tulsa, where her own family was. The man she married was..." She hesitated oddly over that and then continued. "...Someone she'd known before, a widower. They started having more kids right away. I have three sisters." She took a sip from her wineglass, her eyes far away and sad in the soft glow of the big red Christmas candle she'd lit in the center of the table. "I don't feel close to any of them—my mother or my sisters. My..." There was another of those strange hesitations, "...stepfather's okay, I suppose. A fair man.

But not a warm man." She set the glass down, thought a minute, and then took another sip. "The years I was in Oklahoma, all I ever wanted was to come back home, to California. When I turned eighteen, that's what I did.

"I went to Sac State, majored in business at first. I took a drama class as an elective—and just fell in love with it. I mean, with the whole idea of building sets and lighting them and making—I don't know—magic, I guess. I switched my major to Theater Arts. And then, in my senior year, I met Kenneth . . ." Her voice faded.

Burnett prompted, "Your ex-husband?"

"Yes." She refilled her own wineglass. "It was a mistake from the first," she said.

"What?"

"Everything. I was never interested in the performance end of the theater. But one of the teachers talked me into taking a bit part in one of the shows—to round out my perspective, I was told. It wasn't much of a part. I had about five lines. Mostly, I stood around in a cocktail dress looking decorative. Kenneth saw that play. He's a land developer, and he was in Sacramento putting together a deal, and the son of the man he was buying the property from just happened to be in that play, too. Kenneth came backstage after the show, and he asked me out. I couldn't believe a man like that would be interested in me."

"A man like what?"

"A rich man. Older—he was forty-one to my twenty-two. Very sophisticated. In two months we were married and living in his house in the Bay area. For the first five years of our marriage, he completely dominated my every thought and action. He chose my clothes, my friends and the books I read. He made me into his ideal woman...."

"And then?"

She fingered the nest of holly at the base of the red candle and took another sip of wine, sighing as she set the glass down. "And then one day I looked in the mirror and realized I didn't know who I was."

"What did you do?"

"Nothing, for a while. Then I went back to school. Kenneth was furious at first, because he wanted me at home. He wanted me *available* at all times."

"He missed you, you mean? Because you were gone all the time?"

"No, he didn't miss *me* one bit."

"Then what?"

"The way he saw it, I had a job already. I performed a very necessary function. I was Kenneth Dayton's perfect wife. That was a full-time career, as far as he was concerned."

Burnett flinched at her use of the word *perfect*. Amanda had been *perfect*. And she'd made of her wifehood a full-time career. He asked, trying to keep his voice merely curious, "What about children?"

"Children weren't part of it," she said. "Kenneth had a family by his first wife. He wanted a hostess. A dinner companion. An ornament to wear on his arm— when he needed me, which wasn't all that often, really."

Burnett realized he'd been tensing up when he felt himself relax. Perhaps he *had* thought of Amanda as an ornament at times. But they had both wanted a family. In fact, it had been the lack of children, more than any other issue, that had ended their marriage.

Strange. For a moment there he had begun to see a little of himself—the self he was *supposed* to be revealing to Frannie tonight—in the man she had once married. But, of course, that wasn't the case. Not at all. Not in any way that really mattered. . . .

Frannie said, "I'm talking too much, boring you. . ."

"No," he told her quickly. "I was just thinking, that's all." She was sitting to his left, at the head of the table. He leaned toward her, coaxing. "So you went back to college . . ."

"Yes." The dark rims around her irises looked smoky black; the blue centers like a summer sky. "Ned?" she giggled, a sound both husky and nervous.

"What?"

"You're staring at me."

"You noticed. Go on about college."

"Well, I went. To San Francisco State, this time."

"And?"

"And, by the time I had my Master's degree, Kenneth and I were hardly speaking. Eventually, I got my job in Sacramento. I told him I wanted to take it, and he told me that was . . . convenient."

Burnett frowned, puzzled. "Convenient that you wanted to move to Sacramento, when he was based in the Bay area?"

"No, convenient that I was ready to move out of his house. He'd found someone else—someone who appreciated him and the kind of life he was willing to provide for a woman. He'd been planning to tell me for months, he said. He wanted me out so he could move her in."

The summer-day blue of her eyes was cloudy now. Burnett caught her hand. "I'm sorry, Frannie," he said, hurting from the pain he saw in her face. "He was a damn fool."

She bit her lip and shook her head. "You don't understand. I'm not sad because he cheated on me, or even because he replaced me like—like a piece of furniture he'd become dissatisfied with. I'm sad because I was willing to settle for so little when I married him." Her face changed, became less sad and more reflective. She went on. "And now, for the first time, telling you, I feel a little sorry for *him*—believe it or not."

"Why?"

"Because he was the kind of man people envy. He had success and money—and power, too. And yet, I never really knew him in the eight years we were married. I think deep down inside, he was afraid..."

"Of what?" Burnett, feeling uncomfortable once more, released her hand and picked up his fork.

Frannie drank more wine. "Something—I don't know for sure." Her tone was musing; she stared into the candle flame. "I really don't believe he ever loved me. Maybe he didn't know how."

Burnett chewed the last of his steak slowly, telling his tensing stomach muscles to relax. But relaxing wasn't easy. The man Frannie described was just too familiar. In fact, Burnett felt he understood Kenneth as well or maybe better than the woman sitting next to him did—because Kenneth could have been himself. A man good at giving orders, good at taking charge. But empty at the core. A man incapable of loving.

"In any case," Frannie spoke again, setting her glass down and picking up her own fork, "we were divorced, and I moved to Sacramento. And I joined a support group. I'm working on my problems, so I won't make the kind of mistake I made with Kenneth all over again."

"What mistake, exactly?" he asked, his voice gruffer than he meant it to be.

But she didn't notice his tone, only his question. She was still pensive, still absorbed in the why and wherefore of the choices she'd made in the past.

"I found someone distant and domineering," she answered after considering. "A wheeler-dealer who was willing to tell me how to run my life. Then I married him and did what he told me to. It was totally irresponsible of me. I've learned my lesson, as far as that goes. I'll never fall for a man like that again."

The tension in Burnett's stomach twisted into a knot. It had been bad enough to hear her seeming to describe himself when she talked about her "ex." But now she was, all unknowingly, giving him notice: if he told her who he really was, he wouldn't have a chance of getting close to her.

Harmless, ineffectual Ned might be allowed to sit at her table and chow down on her steaks. Sweet, unassuming Ned might kiss her gently in the kitchen and pull her arm through his for a walk to town in the snow.

But Burnett Clinton might as well face facts: if he told her about his real self tonight, he was out of here. And fast. She'd learned her lesson about men like *him*.

"Ned?" Her voice was apprehensive now. She had sensed that his mood had changed.

"What?"

"Is everything okay? You seem a little—"

"What?"

"Are you angry? Is it something I said?"

"It's nothing," he said, wishing to hell she'd just let it go.

"Please, Ned. That's not true." Her voice was quiet, full of steady conviction. "If something's bothering you, I'd appreciate your being honest about it."

Honest. She wanted him to be *honest*. The word turned like a knife inside him.

"Ned . . . ?"

"All right," he said, and stood up. "You really want to know what's bugging me, huh?" He was surprised at his own voice, at the drawl in it. Ned's drawl. He thought, vaguely, that he was sometimes beginning to feel more like Ned than like himself.

Because *she* wanted Ned. And, damn it, of his two selves, Burnett and Ned, he knew damn well which one might have a chance for that fantasy white Christmas he'd been dreaming about.

"Yes." She looked a little frightened at his vehemence, but she didn't glance away. She stared him straight in the eye. "I want to know."

"Fine—you say you'll never love some rich bastard again. Some guy who'll tell you what to do, dominate your life."

"Yes," she told him levelly. "That's what I said. And I meant it, too."

"Then who will you love instead?" he demanded, moving closer and looming over her, anger and frustration clear in every taut muscle of his big body. "Who will you love instead—a penniless beggar?"

Chapter Eight

Frannie stared up at him. Since she didn't know his secret, she misread him completely. She saw his guilty anger as proud defensiveness. She said, "Money isn't the issue, Ned. Not at all."

"Don't give me that," he said. "Money means power. And power means control."

Frannie was bewildered. He spoke with such certainty. Almost as if he understood the things that drove men like Kenneth, loveless men, who lived to dominate and command. But of course he couldn't understand, not in the concrete sense, at least. Not him. Not her sweet, diffident Ned St. Charles.

No, his anger was only a display of frustration, the same frustration he'd displayed when she'd tried to give him a few dollars to help him get home. His pride was wounded. Because, in the world, he was a powerless man, a man who thought himself a failure.

A yearning came on her—to grab his head and pull it down until their lips could meet, to melt his baffled fury with the sweetness of shared passion. She blinked, to try to push away that yearning. Then she said in a torn, breathy voice, "No. It isn't about money. Really, it's not. At least not anymore. I can—and do—take care of myself now. I don't need a man to support me financially. If I loved someone, money wouldn't matter..."

Something was happening in his dark eyes. Like the lighting of a flame, she thought inchoately, as if the husky sound of her voice was a signal, and now both of them knew what would come next. His hand closed around her upper arm.

"Ned..."

Slowly he pulled her to her feet. "Money wouldn't matter," he murmured, "if you loved someone?"

She shook her head, because right then she felt herself incapable of speech.

"What does that mean?" he asked. "Your shaking your head like that—No, that's wrong? Or, no, it wouldn't matter?"

"No, it..." she got out.

"Yeah?"

"It wouldn't matter."

His mouth was slightly parted. In the sculpted male perfection of his face, his lips looked to be the one vulnerable place. They were firmly cut—yet full and soft now, with what she knew in her woman's heart was desire. "If money wouldn't matter, then what would?" he whispered, and he pulled her against his chest.

Frannie felt his warmth and his solidity. Her nipples, beneath the heavy sweater and the bra she wore, grew taut, as if they strained to touch that warmth, to rub against it.

She struggled to remember his question, and it came to her: what would matter, if money didn't?

"A lot of things," she murmured.

"Like?"

"If I could talk to him . . ."

"And?"

"If we had fun together . . ."

"Yeah?"

"If he were gentle . . ."

"What else?"

"And if he had patience, when things got . . ."

"What?"

"When things got tough. If he were . . ."

"Tell me."

". . . vulnerable."

"Vulnerable."

"Yes, that's what I said."

He made a little chuckling noise deep in his throat. And she felt his chest move against her breasts. He still held her arm. The pressure of his clasping fingers was firm and sure through the wool of her sweater.

"Vulnerable." He seemed to find the word amusing. He chuckled again. "And sensitive, too, I suppose. You'd want this fantasy man of yours to be sensitive."

"Is that funny?" She tugged on her arm. He didn't let go.

"No, not really," he said.

"Then why did you laugh?"

"I think you're one romantic woman, Frannie Lawry."

"I am not," she said much too quickly. He'd said it just the way Kenneth used to. Romantic. With a sneer.

"And, what's more, I don't think this fantasy man you're describing is the kind you'd put up with for long."

"What do you mean?"

"The guy sounds like a whiner to me."

"A *whiner?*" She jerked her head back so she could glare at him.

"You bet. So far, we've got this vulnerable, funny, gentle, patient guy..."

"Yes. So?"

"Well, what about reliable? Loyal? What about *responsible?*"

"Yes, well, that too..."

He pulled her close again. "What about *sexy?*"

Frannie swallowed. "Ned..."

"What about sexy?" he asked again, this time in a velvety tone.

"Well, I...yes, of course. Sexy."

He smiled then, slowly. And his grip on her arm loosened. "Of course."

Frannie knew that it was time to step back, away from him. He wasn't even holding on to her now, so it should have been easy. But it wasn't. She stared up at him, thinking how beautiful his mouth was, thinking of the things he'd just said, thinking that perhaps he was shrewder than she'd allowed herself to admit up till now.

He began, very gently, to stroke her arm where he'd been clasping it. It was as if he were petting her, soothing her. And she loved the way it felt.

She quivered, and then drew in a slow breath. "I don't, oh Lord..."

"You don't what?" He stroked her arm again.

"This wasn't supposed to..."

"What?"

"Happen. It wasn't—"

"Yes, it was," he argued sweetly as his hand kept softly stroking her arm. "From the first moment. In the snow."

She felt weak at the core, and remembered she'd drunk three glasses of cabernet. "I never should have drunk that wine." She shook her head. He caught her chin, held it still.

"Okay," his voice was tender. "Blame it on the wine." His hand smoothed her hair. "The moment I first saw you, I thought..." He let his voice trail off.

"What?" she coaxed, and then knew she shouldn't have.

"How beautiful you were. I thought you were an angel. My angel. Sent from heaven to save me from my empty life." His hand traveled in tender exploration down her back, molding her against him, until she felt the strength of his thighs against her own.

"But I'm not," she protested. "Not an angel. Just a woman..."

"Everything's different with you."

"How?" she wondered, not even stopping to think that she was pressing herself against him now, as much as he was holding her near.

"Exciting," he said. "But comfortable, too." His hand continued to caress her back in long, sweeping strokes. "I'm usually pretty...reserved around women."

Reserved. It was an odd word for him to use, she thought. She would have imagined a man like Ned would choose a simpler word—shy, perhaps. Or maybe nervous.

"Angel?" Ned was asking.

"Um?"

His arm held her close, and his free hand toyed with her hair, coiling and uncoiling a long lock of it on his index finger. "Are you still with me? You looked far away all of a sudden." He brought the lock of hair to his mouth and kissed it.

She forgot what she had been wondering about. "I'm with you," she sighed. "Yes."

"Show me," he whispered into the lock of hair.

"How?" she asked, though she knew that was foolish.

He let the lock of hair fall between them, down onto her breasts, which were pressed so firmly into his chest. "Show me with a kiss."

She knew she should tell him no. She asked, "Now?"

He nodded, his face solemn, his dark eyes full of humor and desire. "Now."

"Show you I'm paying attention," she said carefully, as if reciting the terms of a contract so that both interested parties would completely understand what the contract contained. "By kissing you?"

"Yes. By kissing me."

"Now?"

"Now."

"All right," she agreed. It seemed, right then, utterly logical. He lowered his head as she raised hers. It was less than an inch in distance, anyway.

Their lips met; they sighed in unison.

Her heart beat faster. All wisdom hung suspended on a slender thread of delight.

She slid her arms up around his neck. She stroked his hair, holding him close as she felt his tongue tease her lips.

Frannie sighed again, pressing herself ever closer to his body, rubbing her breasts against his chest, so that her already sensitized nipples hardened even more.

His tongue slid lightly along the line between her lips. She parted for him. His tongue slipped inside, just a flicker for a brief moment—and then it was gone.

"Ned..." She opened her mouth wider, inviting him. And he accepted the invitation with a low groan, pulling her tightly against him, kissing her harder and more hungrily.

Then, for just a fraction of a second, her heavy eyes fluttered open and she caught a glimpse of the two of them in the old, gilt-framed mirror above the sideboard. Herself and Ned. Locked in a passionate embrace.

Beautiful. Dangerous. Exactly what she had told herself must never happen. It had to stop now....

She slid her hands to his shoulders and gave a push. "Stop..."

He groaned, very low, but lifted his head. His dark eyes came open, charged with heat and hunger.

"Please. Ned..." she managed to whisper, a hollow, raspy sound. She was still pressed against him, though her hands were braced at his shoulders. "Please. Stop," she made herself say.

Very slowly, he slid his hands along her arms. When he had her by the wrists, he gently backed away.

As soon as the solid warmth of his body no longer supported hers, Frannie let her knees give way and sank into her chair. Ned released her completely and stood there, unmoving and silent.

Frannie sighed and closed her eyes, feeling infinitely weary—weary with herself, because she seemed to keep telling herself how she intended to behave, and then doing the opposite the minute she got the chance.

Frannie opened her eyes again, and found herself looking at the braided pattern of the big, oval rag rug beneath the table, as well as the toes of the beat-up boots that belonged to the man who'd just kissed her. She forced herself to lift her head and face him.

Watching her, Burnett ached for her, for the confusion he saw in her eyes. He longed to reassure her—almost as much as he longed to reach out and grab her and pull her against him once more.

"I don't know what's wrong with me," she said.

"Angel, there's nothing wrong with you. Nothing at all."

"I hardly know you." She looked away, and then back. "I...don't normally throw myself at men I hardly know."

As if he were an actor playing a role that had begun to fit him like a second skin, Burnett said what Ned would say. "What you mean is, I'm not good enough for you."

She made a protesting noise, but he put up a hand. "Let's get real about this," he said. "You'd be a fool to get involved with me. I'm some loser you helped out—but not someone you'd ordinarily *kiss*."

"Oh, Ned..." There was real pain in those beautiful eyes.

"Angel, it's all right," he said gently, and he meant it. Both as Ned and as himself. "I don't blame you for being confused. Damn it, I'm confused, too." He raked his hand through his hair, considering, wondering how to convince her she could trust him without telling her the truth about himself and losing any chance he might have with her.

The moment of thoughtful silence cost him dearly. Because it gave her time to remember her original objective.

She said, "Ned, you have to go. Now." Her voice was flat and final.

His heart felt suddenly dead and heavy as lead. "Frannie—"

"I mean it. No more whys or wherefores. You're right. I don't want to get involved with a man who's got the kind of problems you have. Even you yourself just said that would be foolish of me. But I *am* attracted to you." She made the confession in a self-castigating tone. Then she hurried on, "So the best way to solve the problem is for you to leave as you promised you would."

For agonized seconds Burnett had no idea what to do. For the man he'd always been, after all, there were few options at this point. He held no power over her, so he couldn't demand she allow him to stay. And if he simply refused to leave, he was sure it would get him nowhere at all. She had the look of a woman who'd made up her mind. If he tried stonewalling her, he wouldn't put it past her to contact the authorities and have him forcibly removed.

But then it occurred to him—Ned was *vulnerable*. Ned was *sensitive*. Ned could do things that Burnett would consider blatant displays of weakness and irresponsibility. Ned could beg, plead, *throw* himself at a woman's feet . . .

And, to Frannie Lawry, he *was* Ned.

Burnett allowed all the anguish he was feeling to show clearly on his face. He said, in a tormented growl, "Damn it, Frannie—"

And he dropped to his knees before her.

"Don't!" she said, too late.

He looked up at her, pleading with his eyes. And then he reached out, wrapped his arms around her, and laid his head in her lap.

She stiffened. He felt her intention to shove him away. He held his breath and clutched her tightly, holding on for dear life.

He didn't allow himself to breathe again until he felt the hesitant touch of her hand on his head.

"Oh, Ned," she sighed. And her fingers combed, gently, through the hair at his temples.

For a time they were quiet. She continued tenderly to stroke his hair. Then at last, without lifting his head from the cradle of her lap, he said, "I have nowhere to go."

As the words left his lips, he despised himself for saying them—they were an outright lie. Or were they? If he really thought about it, maybe he didn't have anywhere to go—anywhere that mattered anyway.

"Oh, come on, Ned," she said. Her voice was kind, but it carried reproof. "What about that cabin in Graeagle? Are you telling me you can't return there?"

Leaving the cradle of her lap reluctantly, he rocked back on his heels and looked in her eyes. "I need . . . a friend right now," he said.

Her smile was gentle. "Go home to Sacramento, then. You have a friend there—what's his name?"

"Burnett." He uttered his own name grimly.

"You could share with him how you're feeling."

He tried to keep from looking pained. "I don't think I really explained about Burnett," he said carefully. "He's done a hell of a lot for me, but he's not the kind of guy anyone can talk to. I might as well . . . lock myself in a room and talk to myself as talk to him."

"Why do you say that?" She looked bewildered. "If he's your friend—"

"It's simple," he said in a preemptive tone, wanting to leave the subject of his real self behind before he got himself into more trouble than he could get out of. "Burnett's done all he can for me. But he's pretty fed up with me now."

"You've been lying to me, haven't you?" she asked then, causing his heart to leap disturbingly inside his chest.

"What do you mean?" he stalled.

She sighed. "Oh, Ned. Earlier, you said that Burnett had given you time off until the end of the year."

"Yes," he said warily. "I said that."

"Tell me the truth. Do you still have your job with him?"

His heart settled back into a regular rhythm. She only thought he was lying about having a job. "Let me put it this way," he hedged, "if I come back in better shape than I left, he'll give me another chance."

She shook her head. "Set your stubborn pride aside and be straight with me. What you mean is, you really don't have a job at this point, right?"

Instead of answering, he took her hand and raised it to his lips. He spoke against her fingers. "I'm sorry, damn it. I know I misled you before." *Just as I'm misleading you now*, his conscience whispered.

He pushed the nagging of his better self from his mind. "Let me stay. For a while. Please."

He watched her face soften. She drew a deep, unsteady breath. Then she shook her head, slowly, and pulled her hand from his grasp.

"I told you. No." She started to stand up.

"Wait!" He cast about desperately for his next move.

"You have to go."

"Just listen, please. Just hear me out...." If he hadn't been so frantic to get her to listen to him, he probably would have laughed out loud at himself about then. Burnett Clinton had always made it a point of honor never to beg anyone for anything. Yet, with this woman, he was on his knees most of the time. With his angel, he had no shame whatsoever.

He held her gaze desperately, doing his damnedest to communicate with his eyes and his imploring expression that there had never been anyone as vulnerable and sensitive as he was—not to mention patient, fun to be with, easy to talk to, and kind....

He had to restrain himself from crowing in passionate triumph when she finally said "All right" and sank back to her chair.

Burnett realized then that he had absolutely no idea what it was he just *had* to say. Casting frantically about for something—anything—he played the moment for all it was worth.

Still sitting on his heels, he laid his hands on his thighs. He looked down at them, as if contemplating the weight and deep meaning of what he was about to say. He closed his eyes, praying as he never had in his life that an idea would come to him. Absolutely nothing did.

When he felt he could stall no longer, he looked up and captured her gaze once more. He said the first thing that popped into his head.

"I need you right now—"

"Ned, I—"

He raised his hand for silence, opened his mouth and forged boldly on. "But, er, not the way you might think."

She gave him a puzzled look, scrunching up her adorable nose. "And what way is that?"

"What?"

"What way do *you* think *I* think you need me?"

He blinked, and tried his absolute best not to show her that he had no clue himself of where he was going with this. He said with great sincerity. "What I mean is what I said."

"But you haven't."

"What?'

"Said it yet." She looked now as though she wondered if he were mentally impaired as well as flat broke and a failure at life.

It came to him, then, where to go with this. He said, with simple honesty, "What I mean is, I'm not talking about any kind of man-woman thing. I want you to understand that. I need you, but in a way that has nothing to do with that."

She made a low, scoffing sound. "Ned, don't treat me like a fool."

"I'm not. I'm telling the truth." He allowed himself a slow grin then. "I have to be honest, though, and say I wouldn't fight too hard if you suddenly invited me into your bed."

She cleared her throat. "That is not going to happen."

"Fine. Like I've been trying to explain, sex isn't the important thing, anyway."

"No?"

"No."

"Then what is?"

He tipped his head, wanting to put this part just right. "That it's Christmas," he finally told her. "And that we're both alone when we could be together—as friends only, if that's what you want. I could keep the fires going, and do any odd jobs you can think of to pay for my keep. I can stay in the basement room, just like I did last night." She still looked at him doubtfully. He added quickly, "And it would only be for tonight, tomorrow, and Christmas. I'll leave on the morning of the twenty-sixth, before noon."

Frannie was silent. He knew he was reaching her. She still felt she should keep saying no, and yet she was a kind person, and generous, too. To a giving person like his angel, what he asked wasn't that unreasonable.

"Look," he went on, shamelessly playing on her tender sensibilities. "Lately, I've had to start facing all the ways my life just isn't working out anymore. I need to change some things, but I'm not really sure yet exactly what they are. I feel that if I can just get through Christmas, I'll make it out the other side. I'll be able to pick up the pieces of my life and start over. But I just don't know how I'll stand it, if I have to spend this holiday alone." He subsided, looking noble, he hoped—and yet needy at the same time.

He thought he'd convinced her. But he discovered he wasn't home free yet, when she asked, "What about your brother? Can't you spend the holiday with him?"

He thought about that, and decided to stick as close to the truth as possible. So he said, "Yes. Casey would welcome me. And so would his wife. And my mother— she'll be there, too. They'll be glad to have me."

"Well, then?"

He considered, and went on, still more or less honestly, "They'll spend the whole holiday worrying about me. I'm having enough trouble right now trying to deal with all the ways I've messed up my own life. Having to watch the people I care about agonizing over my problems, too, is more than I can take...." He let his voice trail off, and then decided he had no more to say, so he bent his head—humbly, he hoped—and looked at the rug he was kneeling on.

Frannie, trying diligently to be sensible, gazed down on his bent head. She knew she absolutely must stick by her resolution that he should leave—and yet she wanted, more than anything, to allow him to stay.

All her instincts told her, as they had from the first, that Ned was a good, gentle man. And she completely sympathized with his need to share Christmas with someone on this first year as a single man again.

Last year, her first as a single woman since her marriage, had been hell for her during the holidays. She'd been grateful to have this old house to come to, and Aunt Bonnie to share Christmas dinner with. She understood how Ned could feel the same way on *his* first Christmas on his own.

Also, she *did* like him. Her own Christmas would be much improved, should she have a friend to share it with....

Friend, that warning voice in her head scoffed. *There's a lot more than friendship going on here.*

Well, so what if I'm attracted to him, she argued back in her thoughts. That doesn't mean I have to do anything about it. He said it would be as friends only, and that's just how it *will* be.

Don't be an idiot, Frances, she could almost hear Kenneth jeering. *He's a nobody who can't even hold a job. Send him away now....*

And, of course, she knew what Aunt Bonnie was going to say. *What has happened to you, Frances? Have you lost your mind?*

Christmas dinner would be held at Bonnie's house. Like last year, Bonnie would roast a huge bird, and invite a few of her friends from Downieville and Sierra City, too. That would be an experience—Aunt Bonnie and her lifelong friends. And Ned, the raggedy man from Sacramento, by way of Graeagle and the St. Charles Place bar.

"And where are you from, again, Ned?" one of Aunt Bonnie's friends would politely inquire.

"Oh, Frannie found me drunk in a snowbank three days ago. She took me in and sobered me up and then said I could stay in the basement for a while—would you pass the peas, please?"

"Frannie?" Ned asked softly, interrupting her imaginings. "Are you all right?" He'd raised his head and was looking at her with mingled entreaty and concern in his eyes.

"Yes. I'm fine. Just thinking."

"And . . . ?"

She studied him as he knelt there before her. He looked hopeful and vulnerable and utterly harmless.

"All right, you can stay," she told him at last.

Burnett, stunned for a moment that his fervent wish had been granted, almost blurted out, "Are you *sure?*" He stopped the words just before they escaped his lips and murmured instead, with humble and quiet dignity, "Thank you."

"But there is a condition," she said.

"Name it."

"I don't want to control your behavior for you," she began hesitantly, "but I'm not willing to have someone around who can't stay away from the bar. How bad a problem is alcohol for you?"

There was no hesitation in his reply. "Tell you what," he said. "I freely give my word not to have a single drink while I'm staying in your house. And if I do, then you promise me that you will kick me out right away."

"As if it were that easy getting rid of you," she said with good-natured grimness.

He looked at her levelly. "I mean it, Frannie. I won't have a drink. If I do, you ask me to leave and I will."

She shook her head. "Why is it I believe you when the things you say about yourself seem so vague and hard to pin down?"

"Because, about this, I'm telling the absolute truth."

"Meaning there *are* things you're not being honest about?"

"Everyone has secrets, Frannie," he said soft and low.

He was thinking, though she couldn't know that, that his deception was fully justified. Right now, his angel wouldn't be able to accept his real self. Later, after she knew him better, he would tell her everything.

But not now. Now he would be the penniless, unassuming Ned St. Charles, willing to chop wood and fix anything that broke for a comfortable place to sleep and some nourishing food.

He'd be a nobody, a failure. And as he looked into his angel's glowing face, he found himself thinking that being a pitiful loser for a few days might be the best thing that ever happened to him.

Chapter Nine

"Come in, dear." Bonnie pulled open the door and gestured Frannie into her house.

Frannie held out the empty plate. "No, I won't stay. Here. The fudge is incredible—as always."

"You ate it *all,*" Bonnie demanded in disapproval. "Already?"

Frannie understood that her aunt was still sulking from their last confrontation the day before and spoiling for a fight. Frannie chose not to give it to her.

"No, Aunt Bonnie," Frannie said. "I ate two pieces, put the rest on a plate of my own, and washed this plate, so I could return it. But even if I *had* eaten it all, that is why you gave it to me, isn't it? To eat?"

"Well, yes, of course," Bonnie said. Then, "Oh, why are we arguing?"

"Are we?"

"I don't want to argue."

"Great. Let's not."

Bonnie's little mouth pursed. "Fair enough. No more arguing."

"Fine." Frannie steeled herself for what she planned to say next. Returning the plate wasn't the main reason she was standing on her aunt's front porch. It was Christmas Eve morning, and she could waste no more time in informing Bonnie that she wanted to invite another guest for dinner tomorrow night—Ned St. Charles.

"Is *he* gone yet?" Bonnie asked right then, causing Frannie to wonder if perhaps her aunt could read minds.

"Aunt Bonnie—"

"It's a simple question. Answer it."

"All right. No."

"Good God."

"Aunt Bonnie—"

"Have you lost your mind? What's wrong with you?"

"Nothing, I—"

"Some bum off the street. It's a downright scandalous shame."

"Aunt Bonnie."

"I swear, I just don't know what has happened to you. First Kenneth Dayton, now this. It's...self-destructive, that's what it is. You have no respect for yourself, to get mixed up with—"

Frannie had had enough. "Stop," she said, her voice carrying an unmistakable note of command. Bonnie actually fell silent.

"Now," Frannie continued, "I am allowing Ned St. Charles to stay for Christmas at my house." Bonnie gasped. Frannie gave her a sharp look, and Bonnie remained silent—much to Frannie's surprise. "I understand that you don't approve of that, Aunt Bonnie. And your approval is your business. It's still my house, as I've already told you. And I choose to let Ned stay in it for a few days.

"Now, as for Christmas dinner, I would like to spend it with you and your friends, as we did last year. But I want Ned to be included. He's a man alone, who could use a little human kindness—especially considering the real meaning of the day. May I invite him?"

Bonnie's mouth was hanging open. She snapped it shut, then sputtered, "Why, I . . . I—"

"A simple yes or no will do."

"I don't...can't..." Bonnie began sputtering again, but then caught herself. She drew her stout body up as tall as it would stretch and declared, "All right. Bring him along, then. Though heaven knows I think you are making the biggest mistake of your life."

"Thank you, I will," Frannie said with a pleasant smile, and then turned and marched back down the steps before her aunt could say more.

At her own house, she found Ned down in the basement just screwing the back onto the old clothes dryer, which had given up the ghost sometime yesterday in the middle of drying his shirt and overalls.

"It's the belt," he explained as he pushed the dryer into its place against the wall. "It slipped loose. I readjusted the pulleys and the thing should work—for a while. But what you're going to need is a new belt sooner or later."

"Okay." She stood at the base of the stairs as he turned the dryer on and showed her that it did, indeed, work—for the time being at least. After it ran for a moment, he pulled open the loading door to toss in his clothes, which were waiting in a wet heap on top of the washer. He punched the start button and the dryer began spinning once more.

"How'd it go?" He straightened up and then leaned against the dryer, crossing his hands over his chest. "With your aunt?"

"She's concerned that I've lost my mind—and you're invited for Christmas dinner."

"That should be interesting."

"At the very least." She chuckled, and then fell silent. The rumbling of the dryer seemed to swell to fill the space. "Ned?"

"Yeah?"

"If you think you could trust me, I'd like to know. About you. And your family. And even what happened in your marriage...." Frannie spoke haltingly because across the concrete floor, he was scowling at her. She rushed on, before his dark look could intimidate her into silence. "I've been thinking about what you said last night, that everyone has secrets. Maybe that's true. But it seems to me that you've got more than most people."

"What do you mean?" he asked. His tone was cold, as if it could freeze her out of asking more questions.

She forged ahead. "Well, I can't put my finger on it exactly, but when you talk about yourself, I feel like you're hiding something."

"I am," he said flatly and held his hands out, palms up. "I told you that yesterday."

"It's not enough. If you won't trust me, it makes me wonder if there's something about you I really should know. Have you done something illegal? Or is someone after you?"

He glared at her. When he finally spoke, he didn't answer either of her questions. "My hands are dirty, and it's cold down here. Let's go upstairs. I'll wash up."

"But Ned—"

"We'll talk," he said with a sharp wave of his hand. "Upstairs. After I'm cleaned up."

"All right," she agreed, "that's reasonable."

"Let's go, then." He came away from the dryer and started toward her for the stairs. She turned and went ahead of him, feeling apprehensive at how brusque and cryptic he had been when she'd only asked him to talk a little about himself.

He spent several minutes in the bathroom. When he emerged, he was smiling.

"How about if we sit in the front room?" he suggested. It was as if, she thought nervously, he'd given himself time to think about what she'd asked of him, to decide how much—and what—he was going to tell her. And now that he had decided how far to go, he could relax a little, smile, be friendly with her.

Frannie pushed away the ugly idea that he might be planning to give her nothing but lies. "Sure," she said, and they went through the dining room together.

They sat on either end of the old, fat sofa. He hitched up a leg and turned toward her. "Okay, what do you want to know?"

A part of Frannie didn't want to push him, wanted to simply say *never mind* and let it go. But she'd gone this far. She boldly inquired, "How about your ex-wife?"

At the other end of the sofa, Burnett considered her question.

He'd resolved, as before, to try to stick as much to the truth as possible, and not to volunteer any more than was necessary to keep his angel from deciding he was too secretive about himself for her to risk having him around. Now she was looking at him expectantly, licking her lips a little, nervous and adorable. He stalled, "What do you want to know about my ex-wife?"

"Well . . . who divorced whom?"

The truth, as much as possible, he reminded himself. "She divorced me."

"Why?"

"She wanted kids. I couldn't give them to her."

Frannie now wore a sympathetic expression. "You aren't able to father children?"

He shook his head. "With most women, according to all the doctors we saw, there should be no problem."

"I don't understand."

Burnett was beginning to wonder if he should have stuck so close to the truth after all. The medical explanation for his and Amanda's fertility problems was complex.

"Can you explain?" Frannie prompted.

Burnett dragged in a deep breath. "It's real...complicated."

"Just try. Please."

"All right." He paused for a moment to organize his thoughts. Then he began, "What we were told is that our body chemistries were too similar. See, an embryo is actually a foreign body within the mother's body. And the natural reaction of her body is for her white blood cells to attack and destroy it. But, in normal cases, when pregnancy occurs, the mother's body also begins producing what are called blocking antibodies—antibodies that wipe out the attacking white blood cells, so that the embryo is protected from destruction by its mother's immune system."

Frannie, Burnett noticed, was looking a little dazed. He allowed himself a shrug. "I warned you it was complicated..."

"Go on, I'm following. More or less."

"In our case—Amanda's and mine, I mean—the doctors believed that our body chemistries were just too similar. Amanda's blocking reaction was never triggered, because her system didn't recognize enough difference between the embryo and her own body. But her immune system *did*. So it attacked and destroyed the baby in the first trimester whenever she got pregnant."

"And how often was that?"

"Twice, that we know of for sure. She had two mis-carriages before she was three months along." Burnett was silent for a moment, watching Frannie's face, wondering if he'd made a mistake trying to explain all this. Ned was supposed to be a simple guy, not at all the type who tossed around words like *embryo* and *anti-body*.

But Frannie, as usual, was more concerned for his pain than his inconsistencies. "Oh, Ned. I'm sorry."

The tender understanding in her voice struck a chord deep within him. He found himself opening up per-haps more than was safe. "She wanted to be perfect," he said. "The perfect woman. The perfect wife. And part of being perfect was producing perfect children."

"Adopting wasn't an option, then?"

He thought about that, and found himself telling a little more of the truth. "When my sister died, leaving her son, Mike, alone, Amanda wanted him. But my sister had wanted Mike to be with Casey. Amanda and I fought pretty dirty in an effort to get Mike."

"That was the 'family crisis' you mentioned be-fore?"

"Yes. But Casey won. Mike stayed with him in the end. And it was the right thing. I understand that now."

"Why?"

"Casey was—is—a much better guardian than I ever would have been."

"Casey has money?" Frannie's look was full of gentle compassion.

"Money enough," he answered, knowing what she'd assume from that. She'd be sure that Ned hadn't been able to afford a lawyer to take the battle to court. It hadn't been like that at all, of course. The real issues had been about emotional suitability as a guardian. In the end, Burnett had been forced to realize he lacked certain qualities that Casey possessed in abundance— qualities like patience, tolerance and a sense of humor.

"In a way," he said, pondering out loud, "that was the real end of our marriage. When I stepped aside and let Casey have Mike. Amanda never forgave me for that. She'd had one miscarriage before the fight over Mike. And then she had the other afterward. That was the final blow. I was a complete failure in her eyes. I couldn't get my sister's boy for her to raise, and I couldn't give her a baby of her own."

"So she left you?"

"Yes."

"Where is she now?"

He shrugged. "Planning to remarry, from what I understand. She might even have done it by now. He's a lawyer, the one who handled her divorce from me."

"So this one's a lawyer. He has plenty of money, I imagine," Frannie commented. Burnett said nothing, though he understood her remark was predicated on the assumption that *he* didn't. She added, "And I imagine she's pregnant."

Surprised at her perceptiveness, he shot her a look. "How did you know?"

A sad smile curved her mouth. "The woman you've described would want to get pregnant *first* this time around. She'd learn from her mistakes."

"Mistakes like me, you mean?"

She reached down the length of the couch and gave him a playful nudge. "Don't get all gloomy on me."

"I'm not gloomy," he said. "Why should I be gloomy? My family considers me unfit to care for my nephew, and my ex-wife was scouting out new sperm donors before the ink was dry on our divorce papers. But that's okay. I'm cheerful. I refuse to let it get me down."

She laughed. "That's the spirit." Then she grew serious. "You said day before yesterday, when I found you in the snow, that maybe you never loved her."

"Amanda?"

"Mmm-hmm."

"I don't know..." He had to struggle to find the words. "I have this...problem about love."

"What problem?"

"Well, I mean, what is it?"

She laughed. "Love?"

"Right."

She looked away, at the Christmas tree across the room in front of the window. Her legs were folded beneath her and her slim body turned toward him. She wore black stirrup pants, a big red sweater and red socks. She must have left her boots outside on the porch, because she'd been in stockinged feet since she came to find him in the basement.

A spark popped in the grate. She jumped, gathering her tucked-under legs even closer.

He asked, "Did you forget the question?"

She looked at him again. "No. No, I didn't forget."

"Well?"

"I don't know if I could give you a . . . definition of love. But I could tell you what I think of, when I think of that word."

"What?"

"My dad. When I think of love, I think of my dad. He loved me, I'm sure of that. And he knew how to show it, too."

Burnett made a low sound. "What about your mother?"

"We aren't close," she said, and the words had such a final sound that he didn't pry further along that line. She gave him a playfully warning glare. "Don't dare ask about *my* ex. Remember, I told you I don't think Kenneth knew how to love."

"I remember."

"What about *your* mother?" she asked. "She's still alive, right?"

"Yes?"

"Does she love you?"

Burnett thought of his mother, Lillian, of her honesty and her strength. Though she'd loved his father deeply, she hadn't let it destroy her when he left. She'd taken her children and a small trust she'd received from a bachelor uncle, moved to Sacramento and opened an ice-cream store, the first Chilly Lilly's. He admired his mother. "Yes," he said, and couldn't resist smiling as he added, "My mother loves me. There must be some hope for me, right?"

She chuckled at that. "And your father?"

"He's dead," Burnett said. "Long dead."

She straightened her spine a little. "You should hear your voice. You sound like you hated him."

"I did," he said flatly.

"Why?"

He told the truth; it could have been Ned's truth, as well as his own. "My father left us when I was eleven. Deserted my mother and brother and sister and me. He left a note that I found. It said that married life was stifling him. *Stifling*. And that he was through with it, for good and all. I never saw him again. Occasionally he would write to my mother. She never divorced him, so she was notified when he died."

Frannie, quiet understanding in her eyes, reached across the distance between them to put her hand on his arm. Her touch was warm. And welcome.

He put his hand over hers. She didn't pull away.

At that moment he was absolutely sure that they would be much more than friends before he left her house. He could see it in the softness of her face when she looked at him, in the way her body yearned toward his—as his yearned toward hers—across the cushions of the old couch.

He squeezed her hand, she squeezed his back, and then she seemed to realize that perhaps she was getting too close. She pulled her hand from his with just enough reluctance that he had to hide a knowing smile.

"What else do you want to know about me?" he asked after a minute.

She shrugged. "I guess that's enough—for now."

They were quiet for a while, then. Frannie rested her head against the back of the couch, and she stared beyond him into the dancing fire in the grate.

Eventually she spoke. "I'll go down and check on your clothes."

"No." He moved to stand. "I can do it—"

She smiled, already up and moving. "Stay there. Enjoy the tree. I'll be right back."

He sank back on the couch as she disappeared around the corner. He thought about what had just happened between them—by mingling truth and lies, he had brought her closer to trusting him. The idea did not make him proud.

Yet, he told himself defiantly, it was the only way. She would never let him get close if she knew the whole truth.

What he needed to do, he realized clearly now, was to get her to make love with him. For a woman like Frannie, making love with a man would be a turning point. She wouldn't give her body without her heart coming along, too. After they made love, she would feel committed to him. Then, very gently, he could reveal the whole truth. She might be upset with him for his deceptions, but she would come to accept him as he really was. After she'd given herself physically, her feeling of commitment would be stronger than her fears.

"They're still damp, but the dryer's working great." Frannie cut short his tender scheming as she came back into the room. She held out his old coat, and had hers over her other arm. "I have some last-minute shopping to do. Want to come along?"

He nodded and stood up, thinking that if he could slip away from her for a few minutes, he might call his brother and Leland Fairgrave, his lawyer. The call to Casey would reassure his family that he was all right.

And Leland could assure Burnett himself that all was going smoothly in his business while he was gone.

Burnett reached out to take the coat from Frannie. She extended it—and with it several folded bills. It took him a moment to register that she was trying to give him money again.

"I told you. No," he said.

"For fixing the dryer," she coaxed.

"Frannie—"

"Oh, come on. It's no big deal. And you have to have a little pocket change, after all."

He looked at her, ready to tell her no again—and then decided she was right. Even the perennially poor-but-proud Ned would probably give in and take a few bucks from her at this point.

"All right," he said. "But I *will* pay you back."

"Fair enough."

He stuck the money in the back pocket of the jeans she'd given him and felt the bent corner of his driver's license as he slid his hand in there. He'd taken the license from the jacket yesterday afternoon, thinking it would be wiser to keep it on him, where she wasn't likely to find it and discover just how *close* he and Burnett Clinton actually were.

"All ready?" She was lifting her wonderful, unruly hair out from beneath the collar of her jacket. He watched as she tried to smooth the wild tangle of curls, and he smiled.

He nodded. "You bet."

They went out to the porch, where she paused for a moment to pull on her boots. He waited, looking out at the glittering, ice-pure diamond of a day.

Frannie finished putting on her boots and reached for his arm. As they had the day before, they set off arm in arm for the bridge that would lead them to Main Street.

Chapter Ten

As they went out the gate to the slush-covered sidewalk, Frannie was scheming. She needed to get rid of Ned for a while.

She'd had a brainstorm. Unfortunately it hadn't come to her until *after* she'd invited Ned to come along to town with her. She'd held out that hideous coat of his—and it had hit her like a bolt out of the blue....

It was Christmas! She could get him a present. And the perfect present for him right now would be some decent clothes. She'd get him a new shirt and some jeans and socks and underwear—and a nice winter jacket, for heaven's sake.

And she was reasonably sure he would even accept what she offered. Because she would be firm that he must not hurt her feelings and reject her gifts. It was Christmas, after all.

The problem was, how to escape him long enough to slip into The Ruffled Goose, the store at the west end of Main where such things were sold.

Once they'd crossed the bridge, Frannie smiled and said hi to everyone she passed. Ned walked beside her, not saying much, nodding at the people to whom she gave greetings. Frannie held on to his arm companionably, enjoying the warmth that radiated from his big body—and plotting how she was going to get rid of him for long enough to do what she needed to do.

A possible approach came to her. She paused and looked over at him. "I have an idea."

"Yeah?"

He was so handsome, she thought. And he'd be even more so in clothes that didn't look ready for the ragbag. "We could speed this whole process up a little, if you do the grocery shopping and I do the rest."

"The rest?" he asked.

"Mmm-hmm," she rushed on. "I need some wrapping paper from the hardware store, and a few things from The Ruffled Goose down the street. So what do you think?"

He shrugged. "Fine with me."

She had to hold back a smug smile. This was *easy*. He went right along with her. He hadn't a clue, she could tell by his open expression, of what she intended to do.

"Here." She took his hand and put her grocery money and the list she'd made into his palm, then wrapped his fingers around it. "Thanks. I'll meet you at Downieville Grocery. It's the building over there on the right. Half an hour."

"I'll be there," he said.

Frannie pulled her arm from his and crossed the street, stopping once on the other side to wave and smile back at him. Then she turned and made for The Ruffled Goose at the corner end of the covered sidewalk.

Burnett, watching her rush away down the street, lifted his hand, waving in return too late for her to see it.

After he let his hand drop to his side, he stood for a moment, wondering vaguely what she was up to. But then he decided not to examine the reason for his good luck.

She'd played right into his hands, after all. He had some time alone, and there was a phone kiosk right behind him, against the brick wall of a store.

He charged the call to his home phone, and dialed Casey's house first. Casey picked up in two rings.

"Big Brother?" Casey's voice came at him over the line, a voice with lazy humor in it as well as affection and, right now, carefully masked concern. "You doing all right? Still up at the cabin?"

"I'm doing fine. I'm in Downieville," Burnett explained. Casey would know of the town. They often drove through it when they took Highway 49 to Graeagle.

"What for?"

"I got in the Jeep day before yesterday. I started driving. I wound up here."

Casey chuckled. "That bad, huh?"

"Yeah. Pretty bad. But better now."

"You coming home for Christmas? Joey—" he used his wife's nickname "—made me buy this bird that would feed an army. And Mike's bought you something—I don't know what, but it's wrapped in three different kinds of paper and he swears you're gonna love it." Burnett cleared his throat, touched at the news that Mike had chosen him a special gift. "Also," Casey went on, "Mother's made divinity."

"Divinity," Burnett repeated, rather stupidly, he thought, as he realized that he *did* love his family. If it weren't for his angel, he'd hop in the Jeep and head home.

"Big Brother? You still there?"

"Yeah, I'm here. And I'm staying here for Christmas. And hopefully longer."

"Hopefully?" Casey chuckled again. "Come on, what gives?"

Burnett coughed.

"It's a woman," Casey said.

"All I did was cough."

"What's her name? What's she like?"

"Frannie. Frannie Lawry. She's an angel, I swear. My angel. She pulled me out of a snowbank, so drunk I couldn't walk. And she took me in her house and she's letting me stay. She thinks I'm flat busted. She thinks my name's Ned."

"Whoa, hold it."

"Yeah?"

"You sure you're okay?"

"That's what I called to tell you. I'm fine. I'm in Downieville at Frannie Lawry's house until sometime after Christmas Day. She doesn't have a phone, but all you have to do is ask someone who lives in this town. They'll know her. Everyone seems to know everyone else around here.''

"I don't get it, Big Brother. You *told* her your name was..." After all the years of training, Casey couldn't quite say it.

"Ned. Yeah," Burnett finished for him.

"But you hate that name. After Dad left, you used to beat me up every time I called you that.''

"I know, but it happened. I was drunk and I said my name was Ned. And now..."

"What?"

"That's who I am to her. That's who she thinks I am."

Casey was silent. Then he said, "Advice and a dollar fifty will get you a ride on the bus, but Burnett..."

"Yeah, what?"

"If you aren't honest, get that way. Okay?"

"I will.''

"When?''

"Soon. Listen, freeze me some of that bird and save me some divinity, and tell Mike I'll get that present from him the minute I hit town again."

"Burnett—"

"Really, I gotta go." Burnett depressed the hook before his brother could say more.

Then he stood for a moment, clutching the handset, staring at the silver tinsel on one of the decorated trees that lined the streets. The tinsel moved in the slight cold wind, flickering and glittering beneath the winter sun.

Get honest, Casey had advised.

I will, Burnett swore, both to his brother and to himself. As soon as we've made love and she really trusts me. As soon as I know she won't send me away.

"Excuse me," a voice asked from behind him. "Are you through with the phone?"

He turned to face an old man with a cane. "Just one more call, sir," he said automatically, not even aware that his voice was a soft, gentle drawl and his face wore a solicitous expression. "Will that be all right?"

"You go right ahead, son. I'll get me my smokes from Yo-Ho's here." He pointed with his cane at the brick building. "And maybe when I come out you'll have your business all done."

"Thanks." The old man tottered off, pretty spryly, Burnett thought, for a guy who looked eighty if he was a day.

When the old man had disappeared into the corner store, Burnett dialed Leland Fairgrove. The secretary put him right through.

"My God, Burnett," Leland swore the moment he got on the line. "Where the hell are you?"

"Away. Is there a problem?"

"Jordan McSwain and four of the other franchise buyers are here."

Leland was talking about the key man in Burnett's upcoming franchise expansion plan. McSwain, who years ago had managed a store for Burnett, had done well for himself since then. Now he wanted to invest in Chilly Lilly's. He had a friend who was head of site development for Randall's Supermarkets, a national chain. The plan was that twelve franchise Chilly Lilly's would be built adjacent to twelve new Randall's Supermarkets.

Leland went on, "McSwain and his people need some paper from us. Now. Randall's has decided they want a firm commitment from us before the first of the year, and McSwain needs something official to take to his man in site development."

"Where is McSwain now?"

"I told you. Here." Leland's voice rose a notch.

"Settle down, Leland," Burnett warned. "Everything will be fine. Are you saying McSwain is at your office?"

"No. He was. They came into town last night, and I took them to dinner. I said you were out of town on an emergency, and would be back today."

Burnett looked at his wrist out of habit—before he realized that he'd left his Rolex in Graeagle with his pin-striped suit. "What time is it, anyway?"

"Quarter to noon."

"On Christmas Eve. It's too late to do much today anyway. Is McSwain taking the others to Tahoe for Christmas and the weekend?" It was a logical question. McSwain had originally come from Lake Tahoe. Some of his family still lived there.

"Yes," Leland said.

"I thought so. Where's he staying? Give me a number."

"A phone call isn't going to do it, Burnett. What's the matter with you? This is a hell of a lot of work on the line here."

"Give me the number."

The voice on the other end grudgingly complied.

"Thanks, Leland. Unless you hear from me, I'll be back Monday morning, in your office at eight sharp. We'll get together with McSwain and the others then. We'll write something up to satisfy all of them, and I'll put my name on it and things will be fine."

"Burnett, we need to get together. Go over this. Decide on the wording and—"

"Write it up, Leland. I'll go over it Monday. It will be fine."

"But—"

"Your office, Leland," Burnett said in a voice of steel. "Monday morning. Eight o'clock. Have you got that?"

Leland cleared his throat. Burnett's tone had told him more clearly than words ever could that he was wasting his breath to try to get Burnett to return early. "Yes. All right. I have it. But can you at least give me a number?"

"There's no phone where I'm staying."

"No phone?" Leland sounded as if he might have a stroke. "How can you go someplace where there is no phone?"

Burnett allowed himself a dry laugh. "Merry Christmas, Leland. See you Monday."

"Yes, of course, but—"

Burnett hung up the phone.

He turned, grinning a little, to find the old man, a carton of Pall Mall's under one arm, leaning on a cane and watching him.

"One more call?" Burnett asked sheepishly.

"Well, you just go right ahead." The old man nodded in a rather courtly fashion, and made himself comfortable on a nearby bench. He opened his carton of cigarettes and lit one, drawing on it with obvious relish. Then he coughed into his fist and gathered his heavy coat closer against the chill.

Burnett set about reaching Jordan McSwain at his hotel.

"Jordan? This is Burnett," he said when the hotel's front desk put him through.

"Clinton? What the hell? Where are you, buddy?"

Burnett smiled. Though he and Jordan were as near opposite as two men could be, Burnett had come to like the other man over the years. Jordan was a huge blond giant who loved two things equally—a good time and big deals.

"Gone till Monday," Burnett said. "Unless you absolutely have to have that piece of paper before then."

"So Leland filled you in, huh?"

"Yeah. And it's no problem. He says you're heading up to Tahoe for the weekend. And so I was thinking we all could go ahead and enjoy the holiday—and take care of business come Monday morning."

"Put business on hold and have a good time?" McSwain sounded truly baffled. "Is that really you, Clinton? And if it is, are you feeling all right?"

"Yes, Jordan. It's me. I'm feeling fine. Terrific, as a matter of fact. So what do you say? If you insist, I can be there in two, maybe three hours. We'll get you what you need today and—"

To Burnett's relief, Jordan cut him off. "Aw hell, no. If Burnett Clinton's gonna put pleasure first for once in his life, who the hell am I to spoil the party? I don't have to see my guy at Randall's until Tuesday, anyway."

"Good enough, then. Say, ten on Monday?"

"You got it, buddy. And Burnett?"

"Yeah?"

"Kiss her once for me, okay?"

Burnett chuckled and hung up.

Down on the bench, the old man stubbed out his second cigarette and rose shakily with the aid of his cane.

"Thanks for waiting, sir," Burnett said as he stepped out of the way. "And Merry Christmas to you."

The old man gave the greeting back. "Sounds like some big deal you got cooking there, son." There was a distinct glint in the old codger's pale eyes. Burnett realized he must present something of a contradiction, wearing clothes salvaged from the next rummage sale, and babbling on a pay phone about million-dollar franchise deals.

He winked at the old man, whom he was sure he'd never see again, and allowed his good spirits to carry the day. "Yeah, they can't do without me in the world of high finance."

The old man gave an approving cackle in answer and picked up the handset to make his own call.

Burnett strolled the few steps to the corner of Commercial and Main and then stood for a moment, in a kind of pleasant shock at what he had just done. For the first time in his life, he'd put his personal desires above his professional responsibilities. And it had felt fantastic.

Grinning like an idiot, he calculated that he probably had about twenty minutes until he was due to meet Frannie at the grocery store. He glanced at the list she'd handed him; only a few things. His guess was he could get the things she wanted, and still have a few minutes to spare.

Idly, he scanned the street, noting the post office across the road, and the hardware store next to it. Above the street, as probably could be seen in any number of small, western towns, hung silver tinsel looped in garlands. Down at the entrance of town a silver star wrapped in colored lights hovered proudly between the grocery store and the building across from it, spreading holiday cheer to a wintry world.

Tomorrow was Christmas Day. And he'd be spending it with an angel. The thought brought a warm glow to his cold skin.

Christmas. Tomorrow, he thought. And then it occurred to him that he had no gift to give her.

The noon bell sounded loud and long as he turned quickly toward the gift shop down the street to his right.

The place was called The Mine Shaft, and he went down rough-hewn wooden stairs to get to it, in a basement beneath Cirino's bar. The little shop had two rooms. Burnett concentrated on the shelves and glass display cases in the space immediately beneath the stairs.

He found what he wanted almost immediately—as if it had been waiting for him. A Christmas angel in a snow bubble.

She stood very still and proud in there, her hands tucked in the folds of her belled sleeves. Her robe was white, trimmed with gold. When he turned her bubble upside down, the swirling tiny storm around her sparkled with flecks of golden glitter.

"She's lovely, isn't she?"

Burnett detected the note of nervousness in the clerk's voice. He looked down at his old coat and frayed borrowed jeans, and he understood that the woman was probably wary about a man like him, someone she didn't know who appeared to be down on his luck.

He tried a hesitant smile, and watched her wariness fade somewhat. "She's beautiful, ma'am. How much?"

The woman told him. With tax, it was just a few cents less than what Frannie had pressed into his hand before they left her house.

Burnett beamed, happier at that moment than he'd been in years and years. "I'll take her. Can you wrap her for a gift?" The woman agreed that she could.

Five minutes later Burnett emerged into the thin, bright sunlight with the wrapped angel tucked safely in the inside pocket of his shapeless old jacket. He hurried to the grocery store and was almost through the list Frannie had given him, strolling contentedly down the narrow aisles, when she caught up with him.

She was grinning, and her cheeks were stained pink, whether from the cold or excitement, he couldn't be sure. "How are you doing?" she asked.

"Almost finished," he told her. She was clutching a big shopping bag. He gestured at it. "Why don't you put that on the cart?"

"No, no . . . I'll just hold onto it."

He shrugged and opened the refrigerator case for a half gallon of milk. "Did you get everything you needed?"

"Absolutely. I did."

He turned and gave her a look. "What gives?"

"Nothing. What do you mean? Nothing gives."

They looked at each other for a moment. Then he said "Right" and rolled his eyes in a signal that he had a pretty good idea what she was up to.

They both burst into an absurd fit of laughter.

Nearby shoppers turned to look, smiled indulgently, and moved on down the aisles.

When the shared laughter faded, Frannie said. "It says on the bulletin board by the old theater that there's a candlelight service tonight at the Methodist church. I haven't been to one of those since I was little. Would you mind if we went?"

"I'd love to go," he told her, and meant it, though he was not a religious man. He'd have gone to church every day of the week, as long as Frannie went, too.

"I feel like . . ." she began.

"Tell me," he coaxed.

"It was a good idea," she said, her gaze sliding away and then back. "For you to stay. A good idea for me, as much as you. I'm, well, just glad you're here."

Her lips were slightly parted. He wanted to bend down and claim them with his own. But he didn't. Not yet. Soon enough, he told himself. He was absolutely certain now that his angel was near to being his in every way.

Chapter Eleven

The church was across the street from Frannie's house, and the service began at eight. Burnett felt strange at first, in his old clothes, but Frannie assured him that people came as they were.

They picked up candles at the door, and signed the open register on the podium inside. Burnett felt more than a little reprehensible signing his name as Ned St. Charles—especially within sight of the rugged cross on the altar and the looming pictures of Jesus and his lambs. But he did it anyway.

They sat in a pew near the back, and Frannie waved and nodded at everyone. She had an especially big smile for that mean mother hen of an aunt of hers, who took a seat a few pews up and across the center aisle. The aunt granted her a curt nod—and Burnett a disparaging frown.

There were perhaps twenty-five people there when the service began. Burnett and Frannie shared a hymnal, though they didn't really need to because there were more than enough to go around. Her singing voice was sweet and high, and she kept sliding him glances, coloring sweetly when he intercepted them.

A tide of mingled sentimentality and desire rose up and washed over him. He found himself thinking that sitting in that old oak pew next to his angel and sharing a hymnal was closer to heaven than he'd ever been in his life. When he tipped his candle to hers, spreading the light of the world, he felt himself transfixed by the light that shone from her eyes. It was all he could do not to kiss her right there, in front of the whole congregation.

When the service was over, they left the church arm in arm. In the darkness, a light, picture-postcard snow was falling. He started to cross the street to her house, but she tugged on his arm.

"Not yet. I want to show you something."

"What?"

"A surprise."

He went where she led him, down the sidewalk and around the corner to Pearl Street. He heard the music way before they got there. Tinkling Christmas music.

"What is it?"

"You'll see."

Soon enough, they reached the source of the sound. It came from a two-story house that backed onto the Downie River. The second floor of the house possessed a large balcony, accessed by a sliding glass door. Beneath the gabled roof and framed by the intricate curlicues of gingerbread trim that embellished the eaves, children in costume moved jerkily, like wind-up figures, in time to the chimelike music.

"What is this?" Burnett asked, enchanted.

"Shh, watch," Frannie instructed, shivering a little and holding tighter to his arm.

Up on the balcony, an angel in a filmy dress rode a rocking horse in the middle of a teeter-totter with an elf at either end. Toy soldiers paraded, up and down, in and out. Mrs. Santa sewed a Christmas quilt, and a red-nosed reindeer pawed imaginary ground. Lights of all colors were woven in the eaves and threaded on the railings, while lacy cut-out snowflakes hung from the rafters, turning slowly in the slight, cold wind.

The tinkling tune ended. The costumed children on the balcony froze in a Christmas tableau. The handful of spectators, including Frannie and Burnett, applauded. Then the music started up again, and the children once more came to jerky, wind-up life.

Burnett pulled Frannie even closer and inquired of her glowing upturned face, "Now will you tell me what this is?"

"The Music Box," she explained. "The lady who lives in this house puts it on every year. The local kids perform in it. It's always a big hit."

They stood for a while longer, watching the children on the balcony as the snow drifted down around them, like a billion tiny frozen feathers, falling slowly to earth. Then they looked at each other.

"Ready to go back?" she asked.

He nodded. They turned together and went back to Frannie's house, pausing briefly on the porch to remove their snow-crusted boots.

Inside, the old house seemed doubly warm after the cold outside. But still, the fire in the front room was low. Burnett added more logs while Frannie chose a Christmas record. Then they settled on either end of the couch, as they had in the afternoon.

The carols played on the old turntable for a while, and neither of them felt any need to fill the space between them with words. Burnett liked that, that he felt so comfortable being quiet with her. Just sitting here as they were, listening to the Christmas songs, he could almost let himself pretend that there were no secrets between them, that she knew him as he really was. And wanted him that way.

Of course, that wasn't true. She wanted him, all right. But she wanted him as Ned. So Ned was what he'd give her, in hopes that in the end she might learn to want his real self.

He watched her, taking in her dreamy expression, her half-open eyes. When she spoke, he let her gentle voice flow over him, knowing a sweet ache of pleasure from just the sound of it.

"When I was a little girl," Frannie told him. "We exchanged our presents on Christmas Eve. Dad would find some excuse to get us out of the house. We'd go to the Forks for dinner, or to church if there was a Christmas Eve service that year. And when we'd come back, Santa would have been here and we'd open our presents." She'd been gazing at the tree. Now she glanced at him, a glint of humor in her eyes. "I always secretly suspected that the reason Santa came early to our house was because my parents liked to sleep in on Christmas morning.''

Burnett made a noise of agreement. "Makes sense." He thought of the gift he'd hidden behind the tree in the late afternoon while she was busy in the kitchen. He leaned a little closer, putting his arm along the back of the couch. "And what about now?"

"Now?"

"When do you open your presents now—Christmas Eve or Christmas Day?"

"Oh," she pretended to think about that, though he suspected she'd had her answer ready all along. "Christmas Eve. Definitely. How about you?"

"I'm easy," he told her.

"Oh, really?" He saw her foot in the red sock inch toward the floor, and he knew she was going to produce whatever it was she'd sneaked upstairs to wrap earlier in the afternoon.

He decided he wanted her to have his gift first. "Stay put," he commanded.

She looked puzzled, but did as he said. He went to the tree, reached behind it, and came up with the box that the lady in The Mine Shaft had obligingly wrapped for him. He went to stand before Frannie.

"Merry Christmas, Frannie Lawry."

He handed her the little box. She looked at it for a moment, as if he'd pulled it from a hat. And then she sighed, "Oh, Ned."

"Open it."

She did, slowly, untying the gold ribbon and carefully peeling away the red foil wrapping paper. When she took the bubble from its nest of tissue, she held it reverently and turned it upside down once. Then she looked through the round wall of glass as the gold and white storm swirled around the figure within.

"She's beautiful." Frannie met his eyes over the globe in her hands. "But she isn't smiling. Do you think she's happy in there?"

She sounded so sad, Burnett thought. He said, "I don't know," feeling hurt himself, suddenly, and far away from her when he longed to be so close. "I didn't think about that.... You don't like her?"

"Oh, Ned ..." She reached out in a gesture that he read immediately as one intended to reassure. "She's a wonderful gift, and I love her." She took his hand and put it to her lips, then held it against her soft cheek, not even stopping to think that the last boundaries between them were dissolving, the walls crumbling away.

"I only wondered," she whispered, still with her cheek against his hand, "what an angel trapped in a bubble would feel like."

He looked down at her shining, wildly curling hair, and tried to hold himself back. But he couldn't, not completely. He laid his free hand on her hair. It felt like spun silk. He stroked it, and she rubbed her cheek against his other hand.

Beneath the buttons of the old jeans he wore, he felt desire stirring. He yearned to tip her head up, cover her mouth with his and guide her gently backward onto the couch.

But he also knew it was probably too soon. He sensed that the way to win her was to allow her to believe she was the one making the moves. And she wasn't quite ready to go that far yet. She wasn't quite ready to take the lead in lovemaking.

But she would be soon, he knew it with every fiber of his being. And she would be his.

The thought excited him more, at the same time as it terrified him. He was not the surrendering kind. But then he remembered that Ned St. Charles was, and he knew that it would be all right.

Frannie turned her mouth against his hand and sighed. Then she pulled away. She looked up, her light eyes shining. "I have something for you, too."

He'd known it, of course, ever since she'd come into the grocery store, flushed and happy, and refused to put her shopping bag in the cart. "You've done too much for me already."

"It's Christmas," she said, both solemn and teasing. "You got me something and I got something for you." She very carefully set the snow bubble on the small table by the couch and then stood up to approach the tree herself.

"This first." She held out a box that looked just about the right size for a shirt.

And it was. There were two plaid flannel shirts inside, one red and one green. "Festive, don't you think?" she asked when he held them up.

He thanked her. But that wasn't all. There were two pairs of new jeans, a quilted jacket, underwear and socks, and a new pair of leather boots, as well.

He shook his head when all the boxes were opened, positive that she couldn't have carried all this in the bag she'd refused to set on the grocery cart earlier.

Frannie laughed at his puzzled expression. "Except for the shirts, I brought everything back here before I even met you in the store," she announced.

"It's too much," he said flatly, knowing exactly how Ned would react and remembering to play his part. "I can't accept all this."

"Ned, please—"

"No, Frannie. This is just too much."

But she refused to hear him. "It is not. It's Christmas. And if you don't accept my gifts, I will be very hurt."

"Frannie—"

She grabbed up the green shirt, a pair of jeans and some socks. "Try these on. Now. And don't argue. I want to see how well I judged your size." She pushed the clothes into his hands, turned him by the shoulders and gave him a shove in the direction of the kitchen bathroom.

He went, to his own surprise, though he was reasonably sure that as Ned, he should have put up more of a fight. But he was tired of wearing rags, and also pleased beyond belief that she would do all this for him, choose him all these clothes, pay for them with her own money, and then wrap them herself in bright paper and shiny ribbons.

It moved him, the way hearing that his eight-year-old nephew, Mike, had chosen him something special and wrapped it in three kinds of paper moved him. It showed thought and care for him alone, a gesture expecting nothing in return but his pleasure in receiving.

For years, in his bitterness and his fear after his father deserted them, he'd been unable to accept with any grace the gifts his family tried to give him. He worked, hard and doggedly, because he somehow felt responsible—the man of the family now—for his father's desertion. He envied his brother and his sister and Joanna, who lived next door to them. He envied their laughter and their freedom and their easy camaraderie with each other—at the same time as he pushed them away whenever they tried to include him in their childish games.

Over the years, when time for exchanging gifts came, he became the one no one knew what to buy for. He received conservative ties. And monogrammed handkerchiefs. Briefcases and wallets and leather appointment books.

After he married, Amanda had him tell her exactly what he wanted, and then she went down and picked it up—at the same time as she bought his gift to her. After all, she reasoned, she knew what she wanted better than he possibly could.

But with Frannie, everything was different. She went down and bought out the store for him, guessing boldly on his sizes, choosing what she thought he'd like.

In the wavy mirror over the claw-footed sink, Burnett adjusted the collar of the new shirt, then he tucked the shirttail into the jeans.

He turned, to look over his shoulder at the top half of himself, which was all he could see in the cabinet mirror. His conclusion was that the clothes fit as well as things off the rack ever fit him. The shirt sleeves were a little short. He solved that problem by rolling them to below the elbows. The jeans were snug, but long enough, thank God. There was nothing at all wrong with the underwear and socks.

He smoothed the tuck of the shirt and readjusted himself inside the jeans. Then, feeling suddenly anxious, wanting her to think him attractive the first time she saw him out of rags, he returned to where Frannie waited on the couch.

In the living room, Frannie sat looking at the angel in the bubble. She was thinking that she would treasure it always, at the same time as it made her a little sad. The angel was trapped in there, in a way, in her bubble of glittering snow.

But Frannie put aside her melancholy thoughts as she heard the soft whisper of Ned's socks on the bare floor between the rugs. She looked up to see him standing there.

Her breath hitched and caught for a moment in her throat. Lord, he looked wonderful. So handsome. Her raggedy man. Sober. Cleaned up. And dressed in new clothes.

She had the oddest feeling, then. As if she had created him whole. As if he never would have existed except for her. She'd pulled a drunk stranger from a snowbank, and in the space of two short days, discovered in him the man of her dreams. It was wonderful. Magical.

She had sensed it from the first, of course. Ned St. Charles was exactly what she needed in her life. She'd fought it in the beginning. But as each hour melted into the next, it became less and less clear to her how she ever could possibly have been afraid of the attraction he held for her.

"Well?" he asked, sounding apprehensive. She realized he was nervous, as if his peace of mind hinged on her approval.

Something inside her heated at the thought. This big, beautiful man was anxious that she would like what she saw when she looked at him.

She rose, slowly, from the couch, and approached him.

He cleared his throat. "Well?" he said again.

A mysterious, purely feminine smile teased Frannie's lips. "You know—"

"What?" It was more a growl than a word.

She couldn't resist touching him. Though the hair above his ear was neatly trimmed, she smoothed it anyway, tracing the hairline. He tensed when she did that, and she found that arousing. His dark eyes grew smoky. His whole body seemed to gather and flex.

"You're so handsome, Ned," she gave out on a long breath.

His eyes narrowed, as if he gauged her intention. As if he wondered how far she was planning to go with this.

And Frannie knew then, with a delicious hollowing-out feeling inside her, that she fully intended to go all the way.

All her arguments and fears and bargains to the contrary, it was as Ned had said. It was meant to be between them. From that first moment in the snow.

She had lied to herself thinking she could—or even wanted to—escape it. He was a good man. And she sensed he would make love to her as she'd never been loved before.

And she wanted that. She was ready for that. For a man like Ned, who was vulnerable and sensitive. A man with whom she could let herself go.

"Frannie?" Ned was asking, his eyes burning into hers.

"Ned," she breathed, coming up on tiptoe. "Ned, what I said before..."

"Yeah?" His breath was sweet on her skin.

"I lied. About us never being lovers. I want..."

"Yes. Say it."

"I want..."

"Come on, Angel..."

"You, Ned. I want you."

"Now?"

"Yes. Now. Tonight." She brushed her mouth against his, once, her body yearning toward his. But they both held back, swaying there, on the brink of surrender to mutual desire.

"Frannie?" He sounded so desperate and hungry, but unwilling to make the move unless she was sure.

That made her only want him more. "I mean it, Ned." She put her hand on his shoulder, clasping it, feeling the strength and hardness beneath the soft, new fabric of the shirt she'd bought for him.

"You have to take the lead," he got out on a ragged breath. "I don't want to wake up tomorrow and hear you say I pushed you into it. It's gotta be what you want, freely given. Nothing else will do."

"It *is* what I want, Ned." She slowly slid her hand over his chest, molding him, feeling him, memorizing his body, because soon it would be hers. "I'm just a little—"

"What?"

"Scared, I guess."

"I understand."

"You do? How?"

"Because I'm scared, too," he confessed. Frannie thought that was wonderful, that he could admit, as so many men never could, his own fears and doubts.

Frannie kissed him, then. She pressed herself against him as she probed at his mouth with her soft tongue, until he allowed his lips to part. She tasted him, sighing as she felt his arms encircle her at last.

He moaned a little, and she held his head, kissing him long and deeply. And then she pulled back and boldly began unbuttoning the green plaid shirt.

He caught her hands. She looked up into his eyes. "What is it, Ned? Don't you want—"

"You know I do." His voice was rough with the promise of what was to come.

"Then what?"

He lifted his head toward the big front windows, where the Christmas tree stood still and proud. "I want more privacy."

She felt her face coloring. "Oh, yes. Of course."

"My bed in the basement's a little small for two."

She laughed then, a husky laugh, and took him by the hand. "Come with me." She started for the stairs in the dining room. He followed behind her, asking nothing more, willing as ever to let her lead the way.

Chapter Twelve

The room she led him to was tucked beneath the eaves above the kitchen. She left him alone there for a moment, explaining shyly that she would take care of contraception.

"We talked about it in my support group," she said. "And I realized that a woman has to be responsible in every way. By that I mean, I'm *prepared,* not that I, um, make love to every guy that comes down the road."

He didn't know whether to chuckle or hug her. "Frannie," he said. "It's all right."

"Okay, good. Well. I'll be right back."

"Good."

She disappeared back down the stairs. He stood in the doorway, waiting for her, gazing at the room where she slept.

The single tall window looked out on the back road and the snow-covered levee where she'd found him—could it have been only two nights before? He saw that he would only be able to stand to his height near the door, because the slanting of the eaves whittled away the headroom all along one wall. The pink, slightly faded wallpaper had tiny flowers on it. The quilt on the bed was a crazy quilt. It reminded him of the ones that were kept on the foot of the beds upstairs in the Graeagle cabin, random swatches of cloth stitched every which way in a patternless mishmash that had always offended his strong love of order.

This quilt, however, didn't offend him. It seemed whimsical, yes, and dizzying. But not the least offensive.

He was still considering the quilt when he felt the touch of her hand on his neck. He turned. Her arms encircled him, and she started kissing him again, pressing her soft body into his, so he once again felt he would explode with the heat and need that pulsed along his every nerve.

Dimly, through the swimming of his senses, he was aware that she was pulling away again. With a soft little sound of pleasure, she tugged him into the room.

She guided him to the double bed, a plain bed with no head or footboard, covered with its ancient crazy quilt.

She gently pushed him down onto the bed, and took up where she'd left off downstairs, unbuttoning his shirt. He watched, hardly daring to breathe, looking down at her slim fingers as they worked the buttons free of the holes.

When she was done and he felt the night air on his skin down the center of his chest, she peeled back the shirt to his shoulders.

She bent, hesitantly, and put her lips to his chest—high up, just beneath the wing of his collarbone. Her lips were incredibly soft against his skin. He hitched in a pleasured breath.

She glanced up, her light-within-dark eyes as starry as a clear summer night. And then, smiling a little in a secretive, feminine way, she tugged his shirt from the waist of the new jeans. She slipped the shirt down his arms and away.

She looked so busy and adorable taking off his shirt, that he dared to reach for her when she was done. He pulled her down on his lap.

She sat across his knees, giggling a little, as if her very boldness was a source of limitless amusement to her. He held her against his bare chest, and guided her head into the crook of his shoulder. She rested there for a moment, and he felt her sweet breath play over his heart.

Then she moved, tipping her head to look into his face. He smoothed her fabulous hair, feeling beneath it the tender shape of her head.

"I don't feel scared anymore," she said, her look as open as an innocent child's.

"I'm glad," he said, and lowered his mouth, covering her lips with his own. She sighed, and her body seemed to relax even more against him. He kissed her, long and searchingly.

And as he kissed her, his hands roamed her smooth flesh, seeking the warmth of her beneath the big red sweater, and finding the marvelous curve of her waist, the individual shape of each rib, and at last, the full, firm swell of a breast.

He cupped the round globe, and when she sighed and pressed herself closer to his hand, he gently slid his thumb between the cotton fabric of her bra and her silky skin. Lightly, with his thumb, he touched the budding nipple and felt it harden more in sweet response.

"Oh, Ned..." She moaned the name against his parted lips.

For a moment he froze, remembering with a cold clarity just how he had deceived her. He was not the man she thought him at all.

But then she asked, sensing his withdrawal, "Ned?" and he melted inside.

"It's okay, Angel," he murmured, raining kisses on her upturned face.

"You seemed to pull away. Are you—"

He didn't let her finish. He covered her mouth with his own again, and she moaned and murmured something impossible to decipher and relaxed fully in his arms once more.

He wanted to get closer to her. He wanted nothing between them. So he began working her sweater up over her rib cage. She assisted him eagerly, lifting her arms, pulling away with a sigh so that he could slip it over her head and off the ends of her outstretched arms.

He paused, then, to look at her, at her slender, pale arms and the full breasts beneath the practical bra, and the wild halo of hair around her sweet, flushed face.

"Angel," he murmured again, and tossed the sweater on the floor by his discarded shirt.

She flung her arms around him, pulling him against her, straining her head back, taunting him with the tender, exposed skin of her neck. He put his lips there and kissed her, as she sighed and pressed herself closer to him still.

His hands roamed her soft curves freely, making short work of her bra, tossing it away to join the growing pile of discarded clothes on the floor. Her un-bound breasts swelled into his seeking palms. She groaned aloud when he cupped them, lifting her body avidly so that he could do as he wished.

He bent his head and kissed her breasts all over, from the full swells of them to the hard, aroused nipples. He sucked the nipples into his mouth, tasting them, find-ing them sweet beyond measure, aware that they hard-ened even more at his passionate attention.

Totally, incredibly abandoned, as no woman he had ever known had been, she began wriggling, moving on his lap—much to his own sensual agony—until she sat straddling him, her head thrown back, still clutching him against her, keeping his hungry mouth at her breasts. He felt the cove of her womanhood through the barrier of the stirrup pants she still wore. She was pressed right against his hardness. He was sure he would explode—without having done more than kiss her breasts and feel the slim, soft length of her rub-bing against him.

But then she was pushing him backward on the bed, and he gave in to her willingly, dropping back against the quilt.

She sat up, straddling him, and he opened his eyes to see her—wildly sensual, and yet innocent—smiling that secret smile of hers.

She put her hands on his chest, touching him hungrily in an erotic massage. He groaned, recalling in a fragmented sort of way what he had decided earlier—that he would surrender to her. So he lifted his arms and raised them over his head, dropping them back against the quilt, giving his body up to her.

His angel took instant advantage of what he offered, sliding her hands up his arms, until she held him, by each wrist, against the quilt. She lowered her mouth, kissing him, her soft breasts teasing his chest.

Burnett groaned as she kissed him deeply. But then she was pulling away. With a hungry growl, he lifted his head toward her when he lost the tender torment of her lips. But she was only slanting her mouth the other way. And she instantly lowered her lips again to kiss him some more.

"I want to kiss you everywhere..." she promised against his mouth. And then she did what she wanted, kissing a burning trail over his chin, down the straining column of his neck, and over his belly, which he couldn't keep from jerking convulsively when the delicate tip of her tongue teased his navel.

He held his breath at what she did next, unsnapping the fly of his jeans and sliding them down his hips. After that, she slipped off his socks, and then her hands were at his waist again, pulling at the elastic of the briefs he wore.

He felt her slight hesitation, then, as if she couldn't quite bring herself to reveal so blatantly the entirety of him. So he helped her, by closing his eyes and flinging an arm over them, letting her see him as willing to give himself up to her tender hands without reluctance. Letting her do as she would.

And she did.

She stripped the last of his protection away, and she touched him. He groaned, and lifted himself off the bed, sure he was going to go over the edge then. But somehow, he held out.

For more of the same. So that later, when he could think again, he didn't know how he had kept himself from coming completely apart. Because she stroked him and made love to him, until he thought he would die of the incredible pleasure she so freely gave. Finally she loved him with her mouth and tongue, until he cried out in erotic agony. Until, at last, he could remain passive no more.

She gave a little husky cry of alarm and of need as he rolled, suddenly, from beneath her, gaining himself the top position. His eyes capturing hers, he stripped away her slacks and panties, and even the thick red socks. At last nothing, no slightest scrap of clothing, kept her from his sight. He gazed down at her. She stared up at him, her beautiful pale body beckoning him, her breasts rising and falling with each agitated breath she took.

He thought—as much as he could think at that moment—of freedom. That with her, as a penniless nobody she'd pulled out of the snow, he was free at last. No longer bound to the treadmill that demanded he buffer himself with money and success in order to protect himself from loss. He was nobody with nothing. And she wanted him that way.

"Ned…" She breathed the name so tenderly, and she reached up a hand to touch his face. "I love you."

She said it simply, there stretched out nude beneath his hands. And Burnett took the words inside himself, knowing he would treasure them always, the greatest gift anyone had ever given him. Love for himself alone.

Liar, the thought came before he could shut it out. *Not for yourself, but for Ned St. Charles. The man you're pretending to be. She doesn't love you, she loves him….*

Frannie stroked his cheek. "Oh my love," she said, her soft lips caressing the sound. "It's all right. There's no need to say you love me back."

"Frannie…"

"No," she slid her hand behind his head, brought his face down to hers and then spoke against his lips. "Please, Ned. Don't make me sorry I said it, don't freeze me out or pull away."

"I'm not—"

"You're thinking," she chided. "And right now is not the time for thinking. Right now…" She took his hand, and laid it on the curve of one soft, full breast. He gasped, she smiled. "…is time for feeling. The best Christmas gift of all. From us. To us. What it all means can come later. Now, it's enough that I love you and you… care for me." She paused, narrowed those enchanting eyes. "You do *care* for me, at least, don't you Ned?"

"Damn it, Angel. You know I do."

"Good then."

She kissed him. And he was lost. Willingly and completely, in the siren sweetness of her mouth beneath his.

He kissed her back, taking control, though neither of them, by that time, cared in the least who gave in each moment and who it was that received.

He loved her with his body, as she had loved him, from head to toe, with his lips and his hands, until she writhed and pleaded beneath him to have all that he could give. With his hand on her, stroking the core of her, he knew her readiness for him. So he rose over her and nudged apart her slim thighs.

She reached for him, guiding him, taking him within her. She wrapped her legs around him, pulling him deeper, sighing yes. He had that incredible, unbearable feeling once more, as he drove for the first time into her softness—that he wouldn't hold out, that he'd spend himself right then.

And this time, the feeling didn't pass. Instead it grew, expanding and contracting, like the hot sweetness of her surrounding him. He wasn't going over the edge, he was teetering there, reeling in ecstasy. It went on forever. And then he went with it, into a vortex of bliss.

She called out the name that wasn't his name, and he pretended that it was. Because being held within her, moving within her, was the most beautiful thing he'd ever known in his life.

He moved slowly at first, because she sheathed him tightly. But as he felt her full acceptance, and the way she moved excitedly beneath him, he thrust himself within her harder and faster. And she matched him, stroke for stroke, as she clutched his back, the hungry, heated sounds she made coming from deep within her, just like his own.

At last, her release came. He stiffened, giving her all of himself as she writhed and bucked beneath him, crying out in complete abandon, letting herself go. Just before she went limp, it happened for him. He knew he'd hit his culmination—and this time he was right.

With a deep, rolling groan that seemed ripped from the deepest part of himself, he thrust into her. And she surged up to meet him, holding no part of herself back.

He spilled into her, for a moment almost passing out from the intensity of it, and she cradled him inside herself, ardent and welcoming, as the world spun away to nothing and then slowly, like something taking form out of thin air, revolved back into being once more.

Burnett went limp, then, and her tight hold became tender. She stroked his back, and his hair, and the side of his face where it lay tucked tight against her, cradled in the satiny crook where her shoulder met her neck.

Her touch was so soothing, so wonderfully fine, that he was flirting with sleep when she spoke.

"Ned?"

"Um?" He lifted his head enough to place a soft kiss on her shoulder, then lay back down.

She went on stroking his hair. "I'm going to stay here for the rest of Christmas vacation, until the day before school starts again—Sunday, the third." Her voice dropped a little, became diffident. "What I'd like more than anything is for you to stay here with me. Could you—would you do that, do you think?"

He thought of the promised meeting on Monday. There was really no way he could get out of it without tossing over the deal. Tossing over the deal would amount to screwing over a lot of people who trusted him, and obliterating his credibility in the business world—not to mention throwing away several million dollars.

Frannie continued, hesitant and hopeful, "I don't really know what comes next for us, Ned. And I'd like to have this, um, special time with you, so that maybe we can figure that out."

He remembered, with a guilty sigh, that now was the time he'd intended to tell her the truth about Ned St. Charles. After they'd made love, when she was supposed to feel bound to him and thus more receptive to the news that he'd been pretending to be someone other than himself since the moment they met.

"Ned?" She was still stroking his hair.

Her gentle hand felt wonderful. Never in his life had he felt so satisfied and so at peace.

Maybe, as he'd assumed, she would be more likely to forgive him now if he told her the truth. But there still remained a chance, and a very real chance, that she wouldn't. That she'd want him out of her life anyway for what he'd done.

And now that he'd made love to her, now that he knew what it was to be buried in her softness, the idea of losing her scared him all the more.

Silently, Burnett Clinton laughed at himself. His own strategy had turned on him. He'd made love with her so she wouldn't send him away when he told her the truth, and then found himself all the more unwilling to come clean with her.

"Ned? Are you asleep?" Frannie whispered against his hair. And then she sighed and settled him more comfortably against her. He lay still in her arms, suddenly aware of the little clicking sounds of the electric clock by the bed as the seconds ticked by.

Soon he felt the even, steady movement of her chest against his ear. He knew she was asleep. He was reprieved from giving her an answer until morning.

Sitting up a little, he grabbed the edge of the quilt and flipped it over them, so they were rolled in it, protected from the increasing coolness in the little room beneath the eaves.

He thought, as he drifted off, that he hadn't fed the fires downstairs. They would be cold come morning and the old house would be freezing. He'd have to lay the fires all over again.

But it was worth it, he decided, not to leave Frannie's side. Any man who got a chance to sleep with an angel would be a fool to risk losing it, no matter how cold it might be when morning finally came.

"Ned?"

He opened one eye. His angel smiled at him.

He kissed the end of her nose and watched her cheeks turn pink, an enchanting experience, especially since they were both still nude under the blanket, all wrapped up in each other, arms and legs entwined.

"Merry Christmas, Angel," he said, and noticed that, once outside the warm shelter of the quilt, his breath turned to mist. "And the damn fires are out," he added. He moved to throw back the blanket.

"Wait." She shivered and held him close.

He chuckled. "What?"

Her skin colored prettily again. "Nothing." She stroked his back. "I just hate to let you go, I guess."

"I'm going nowhere—except to heat this place up."

"I know." Her arms, which were holding him so close, relaxed a little. She looked past him, perhaps out the tall window on the wall behind him. "I just...I can't believe this has happened, Ned. I never thought this would happen. To me."

"This?" he prompted, his heart eager to hear it, though his mind advised caution until he could decide how to tell her he had to leave her on Monday.

She was suddenly shy. "This. Us. Making love. And what I said last night—it was true." She swallowed, and bravely looked into his eyes once more. "I...I love you."

It warmed him to his toes to hear that. He forgot, for a moment, everything but the reality of her slender body against his, her sweet mouth so close. All he had to do was to reach out and cover it with his own.

"Angel," he breathed as his lips found hers. His body hardened, hungry for her. And he decided the heat stoves could wait. He gloried in her eagerness as she readjusted her legs around him, loosing a voluptuous sigh as he found the place he sought.

For Frannie, it was the same. She felt as if they moved as one being, wrapped in their crazy quilt cocoon, sharing heat and passion, oblivious to the cold outside.

Never, ever had she felt like this—with the one boy she'd known intimately as a college girl, or with Kenneth, who had been an expert lover but somehow never touched her soul.

Ned cried out when his completion came, clutching her close and surging powerfully into her. She took what he gave her, avid and hungry as he was, crying out herself as her own satisfaction claimed her in wave after shuddering, delirious wave.

They lay still, at last, holding each other, sharing the last fading pulsations of the greatest ecstasy two people can know.

It was only after he slipped away from her to tend to the fires that she allowed herself to admit the core of sadness at the center of her heart. She had told him she loved him twice—and he had said nothing in return.

She could accept that, she *had* accepted it. He had said he cared for her; he was just unwilling, for some reason, to say he loved her in return. She felt sad, because she understood it was completely possible that he might never truly love her back.

Frannie pushed the sadness away. She would ask him once more, at breakfast, to stay with her through New Year's. Perhaps he'd say yes. And then she'd treasure every moment of the waning year.

Chapter Thirteen

Downstairs, after Burnett had lit the fires, they showered together, taking turns beneath the ancient shower head in the old claw-foot tub. They scrubbed each other's backs and later dried each other playfully. Once dry, they dressed quickly, since the house was still somewhat cold.

They made breakfast. Burnett grilled bacon and fried a few eggs. Frannie made toast and coffee and poured the juice.

They'd just sat down at the table when the tapping came at the side door. Frannie shot Burnett a quick, grim look. He glanced toward the ceiling once and then concentrated on his plate.

"Door's open, Aunt Bonnie!"

Bonnie let herself in and then stood in the doorway for significant seconds, as if deciding what stance to take in a touchy situation.

Finally, Frannie said, "Merry Christmas, Aunt Bonnie. There's coffee if you want it."

"Well." Bonnie appeared to give the offer serious consideration. Then she decided. "I suppose just one cup." She helped herself to a cup of coffee. "I thought I would give you my gift later, Frances, at my house," she said, her back to the table as she filled up a mug.

"Fine," Frannie said.

Bonnie turned, cup in hand, and marched to a free chair. She sat down, sipped from her cup, shot a glance at her niece and then at Burnett. At last, she intoned with excruciating cordiality, "It's not a bright day, but I don't think we'll get more snow."

Frannie swallowed a bite of egg and glanced out the window at the ashen sky. "You're probably right."

There was a massive silence. Bonnie's piercing eyes kept shifting from her niece to the man she considered an intruder and back again.

At last she asked tartly, "What about the pies?"

"I made them yesterday." Frannie gestured toward the small pantry by the basement door, where she'd set the pies to cool.

"Well. Good. And the gelatin salad?"

"In the fridge. I checked it a while ago. It set up just fine."

"Good. The bird's in the oven."

"Great."

Silence again. Bonnie sipped from her coffee. Then she seemed to come to some momentous decision. She set her cup down with a little plop, not spilling any only because she'd already swallowed most of it.

She turned to Burnett. "Well, I've called a friend of mine in Graeagle. She knows *everyone* who lives there."

Burnett experienced a sick, sinking feeling in the pit of his stomach. Had this "friend" identified him as who he really was?

He fought to keep his expression composed, while inside he groaned. He should have explained everything last night, no matter if she *had* sent him away. It would have been infinitely better than for her to find out like this...

"And my friend tells me," Bonnie went on, "that there actually is a family named Clinton who owns a vacation cabin there."

Burnett cleared his throat, and tried to speak noncommittally. "So?"

"So," Bonnie gave out in a grudging tone, "I suppose you're telling the truth about where you were staying, at least."

"Aunt Bonnie." Frannie's voice held clear warning.

The little woman waved her hand. "I know, I know. You've made it very clear—you don't want me interfering. And I have accepted that, more or less. I'm just trying, if you'll realize it, to get along with him. I'm just doing my best."

Frannie set down her fork and confronted her aunt. "I know what you're doing. You're trying to discredit him."

"Why, I—"

"You're checking up on him. He's my guest. And I won't have it, do you hear?"

"Well, what I found out is in his favor," Bonnie huffed.

"It doesn't matter." Frannie's voice was flat and final. "It's none of your affair."

Burnett, who'd experienced a moment of sharp relief when he realized that the older woman wasn't going to reveal the truth about him after all, was now feeling like a stray dog who'd wandered in from the cold. The two women were doing what they had the last time he'd seen them together—discussing him avidly, as if he were either not there or too stupid to understand what they said. He decided that even Ned would get sick of that after a while.

He cleared his throat again, and spoke in Ned's soft drawl. "Excuse me, ladies . . ."

"It has to stop, Aunt Bonnie."

"Frances, I only want what's best for you."

"Ladies?"

"What's best for me is up to me."

"Well, I—"

"Ladies . . ."

"Now, I want your word, Aunt Bonnie—"

"Ladies."

"I only did what anyone who loved you would—"

Burnett had had enough. He put two fingers between his teeth and let out a loud, ear-piercing whistle.

Both women gasped and turned to him.

"I never," Bonnie muttered.

"Ned, what is it?" Frannie exclaimed.

Burnett smiled unassumingly. "Ladies, I don't mean to be rude. But it really gets me down when people talk about me like I'm not even here."

Frannie blushed, realizing, he could see, that she had treated him as less than an equal. "Oh, yes. Of course. I'm sorry, Ned."

"Thank you," he said, humble to the core.

The tough little aunt snorted a few times, and then actually said stiffly, "All right. Perhaps we *were* impolite to ignore you that way. I apologize, as well."

Burnett nodded, and then said to Frannie, "From now on, Angel, I can defend myself." He was completely aware of the way both women stiffened when he uttered the endearment. But he didn't regret using it.

After last night, things had changed between him and Frannie. And even if he couldn't bring himself to reveal who he was to her, he was not going to sneak around behind anybody's back when it came to loving her.

Frannie looked at him levelly, accepting that he refused to hide their new relationship, at the same time as she responded to what he had just said. "You're right, of course, Ned. I won't rescue you again unless you ask me to."

He turned to the aunt. "And as far as what you did, ma'am. Well, I hope you're satisfied now, after what you found out from your friend."

The aunt made a humphing sound. "*Hope* all you want, Mr. Ned St. Charles."

Frannie shot her aunt an irate look, but said nothing.

The aunt relented, then, just a little. "However. Since it's obvious there's nothing I can do at this point about what is going on between you two, we might as well all be civil, at the very least."

Burnett chuckled. Bonnie Lawry was plain ornery, but he did admire her spunk. "Fair enough."

Bonnie stood. "Dinner's at four. I'll expect the both of you around three or so."

"Great," Burnett and Frannie said in unison.

Bonnie carried her cup to the sink and left as she had come, through the side door.

"I'm sorry she's so mean, Ned," Frannie said after the door was closed and her aunt's compact form had disappeared from the porch.

"It's all right," Burnett said. "In a way, I kind of like her. At least you know where you stand with someone like that."

Frannie made a low noise of ironic agreement, and then they finished their cooling breakfast in silence. After that, they cleared up after the meal, still quiet with each other.

Burnett assumed that Frannie was building up her nerve again to approach the subject she'd opened the night before; she was going to ask him to stay until New Year's.

He learned he was right soon enough. They took second cups of coffee into the living room and sat cross-legged before the fire.

"Ned, last night I asked you a question," she began, staring at the flames in the grate.

"Yeah?" he prompted, implying that perhaps he didn't know what she had asked, despising himself once more for the thousand little ways he continued to deceive her in order to protect the central lie of his identity.

She forced herself to face him. "But you were sleeping. And I decided to let it go until today."

"Okay."

"I asked if you would stay here. With me. Beyond tomorrow."

"I see."

"I asked you to stay until New Year's."

"You did?"

"I thought, maybe, it would be a way for us to get to know each other better. To give ourselves some time together. And to see if what we have could end up going anywhere."

"Ah."

She glared at him. *"Ah. I see. Okay. You did?..."* she mimicked his terse responses. "Don't you have *anything* to say beyond that? Do I have to do *all* of this myself?"

She looked so adorable and unsure and vulnerable. He wanted to grab her and kiss her and lay her down on the braided rug before the fireplace. He wanted to undress her slowly, and spread her hair in a fan all around her beautiful face, and to make love to her until she cried for mercy—and accepted it without the slightest irritation when he told her who he really was.

But she wasn't going to allow him to make love to her right now. Now, she wasn't going to do anything with him until he had dealt with her request. This time, there could be no putting his answer off until later. Though his vague responses might have indicated otherwise, his eyes were open and he was sitting up. She was highly unlikely to believe it if he faked sleep right now.

He searched his mind for a way to explain why he had to leave Monday, and came up blank.

When he said nothing again, she made a low, frustrated sound and looked away. He caught her chin. "Don't turn away."

"Oh, Ned." She pushed his hand away and shook her head. "Don't you understand? This is no picnic for me, either."

"I know," he reassured her.

"You do?" She looked defiant suddenly. "*What* do you know about the way I feel?"

"Well . . . You *have* been making all the moves."

"You noticed." It was a shy whisper.

"And maybe you feel you'd like a little help from me."

Her cheeks colored. "Well, I'd like to know where you *are* on this. How you feel about the two of us. Is it just . . . for a little while? Or could it be something more?"

"Angel . . ."

She put up a hand. "That's sweet, what you call me. And I like it. But sweet names aren't enough. I just want to know what this means to you."

"A lot," he told her firmly. "Maybe everything. Who knows?"

"*You* have to know," she insisted, her eyes filling, though he could see she was trying her damnedest not to cry. "You have to know what you want from me, with me, before we can decide what to do next. It seems

like you're *hedging,* Ned. That you're avoiding deciding whether or not to stay with me for the time I
asked."

"I'm not hedging," he said, though that was exactly what he *was* doing—for a completely different
reason than she assumed.

"Oh, Ned." She shook her head sadly, and wiped
away the two traitorous tears that had escaped the dam
of her lids. Then she sniffed a little and straightened her
shoulders. "Ned," she said, reticent but determined,
"I think you have to look at your behavior here."

Burnett blinked. "Huh?" He had no idea what she
was getting at.

"I'm afraid," she went on, her sweet face a portrait
of gentle understanding, "that the way you're acting
with me right now could be symptomatic of all your
problems."

She didn't know how right she was. He asked, "How
so?"

"You're a wonderful man, Ned. You're tender and
kind..."

"Right. And funny and patient and vulnerable and
sensitive. Get to the point."

"I don't want to hurt you."

"Frannie. Just say it."

"But you're... wishy-washy. I'm sorry, but I think
you have trouble making decisions. And maybe com-
mitments, as well."

Burnett, who had taken on the burdens of a man at
eleven, felt irritation rise—then wash right over him
and away. She wasn't talking about *him,* after all. She
was talking about Ned. And she was actually criticiz-

ing Ned, saying things that, if she thought about it, she might recall he himself had pointed out to her the other day.

He was aware of a little thrill of triumph to hear that maybe she at last was discovering that poor, noble Ned had a downside, after all. And then he felt confused, as he realized that he'd been thinking of Ned as a rival—when Ned didn't even really exist.

Frannie was shaking her head. "I have. I've hurt you. I can tell by your silence."

Burnett bestirred himself. "No, it's all right."

"It isn't."

"Yes, it is," he insisted. "And stop apologizing. You've made a good point."

"Oh," she said, somewhat nonplussed at his ready acceptance of her critical words. "Well, it's something to think about anyway."

"Yeah, it sure is."

"And speaking of evasions..."

He grimly said, "Yeah?"

"Are you *ever* going to answer my question? Will you stay here through New Year's or not?"

Here it was again. Back full circle to the original question. And he still had no idea what to say. "Frannie, I would like nothing better than to do that..."

"An answer," she demanded. "Yes or No. Now."

"Yes," he said firmly. Then, "More or less..."

She stared at him with her mouth open for a minute, then she muttered through clenched teeth, "That's it. I have had it." She started to rise.

He put his hands on her shoulders and held her there. "Listen. Just let me explain."

"Either you will or you won't."

"I will."

"Good."

"Sort of."

"Argh." She wriggled her shoulders. "Let me up. Before I kill you."

"Not until you hear me out."

"Let go of me."

"Will you stay put?"

"All right. Just get your hands off."

He released her cautiously, ready to grab her again if she tried to escape. Her expression vitriolic, she backed away and leaned against the couch. "Go ahead, then," she said. "Explain. I'm listening."

"Okay." He looked away and took a deep breath. He let it out.

This is it, he thought. I just can't keep this up any longer. I'm going to tell her the truth...

But then he turned back and looked at her.

If he told her now, it could be the end of it. She could simply kick him out that door over there by the tree...

"Okay," he said again, and forged ahead. "Yesterday, while you were shopping, I..."

"Yes?"

"...I got in touch with..."

"Who?"

"Burnett." The die was cast. He was off and lying once again. "Burnett Clinton."

"Your ex-boss, the one who let you stay at his cabin?"

"Right."

"And?"

"I wanted to check in with him, you know? Because he *has* been really good to me over the years. I wanted to let him know that I left the cabin locked up and everything. And that I'd be back right after New Year's as planned."

"And how did he seem?"

Burnett sought an appropriate ambiguous word. "Receptive," he said. "Very receptive. As a matter of fact—"

"Yes?"

"He really does have a manager's position opening up for me the first week in January."

"Well, that's wonderful, Ned."

"But..."

"What?"

"He, um, wants to meet with me on Monday."

"*This* Monday?"

"Yeah. At eight sharp. He wants to go over a few things with me, he says."

She looked at him narrowly. He wondered if she was about to tell him she didn't believe a single word he said. "Are you sure about that?"

"Er, what?"

"That all he's after is to go over a few things?"

"Well..." He faded off, relieved that it wasn't Ned she doubted, and gambling that his angel would have a better explanation for what Ned's boss was up to than he could dream up right then.

"It's more likely," Frannie told him, "that what he really wants is to check you out. To see if you're back on your feet again, so he can get someone else if he has to."

"Hmm," Burnett said. "You may just have a point."

Frannie gazed at him. "Well? *Are* you, Ned?"

"What?"

"Back on your feet again."

He lifted his chin. "You're damned right."

"Good. So you'll see him on Monday, and you'll have your job back—now what was so mysterious about that, that you couldn't just explain it to me right away?"

I didn't think of it quickly enough, he thought. "I didn't want you to think I didn't want to stay," he said.

"Then you do? Want to stay?"

"More than anything."

"But you have to be in Sacramento on Monday?"

"Exactly."

She sighed, but she was smiling tenderly. "Oh, Ned. It's all right. You can stay till Sunday night, at least. And maybe even come back for New Year's, if all he wants is to see that you're going to be capable of handling the job."

Burnett blinked as he realized she was absolutely right. He'd been so busy trying to figure out how to tell her he had to leave on Monday, that he hadn't let himself think beyond it. He and Jordan McSwain might do a little haggling about the terms of their agreement, but most of it had been hashed out already. It should all be handled in a day—two at the most. After that, there was no reason he couldn't head right back here to welcome the New Year in his angel's arms.

"You know, Angel," he said, allowing his lips to curl in a smile. "You are absolutely right."

"Oh, Ned," she said, then, her eyes misting a little. "Does that mean you'll stay until Sunday, at least? And maybe come back if you can?"

"You'd better believe it." He scooted over to where she sat against the couch.

"I'm glad," she told him, letting her head fall back.

He loomed over her. "Last night, I wanted to lay you back on this couch."

"And do what?" Her voice was husky.

"Guess."

"I have a better idea."

"Yeah?"

"Why don't you show me." She pulled on the collar of his shirt. His mouth covered hers.

They kissed for a long time, and when he pulled away to give them both a breath, she murmured, gesturing at the front window. "We still have a privacy problem." He groaned, but then she added, "We could simply close the curtains, you know."

It seemed a fabulous idea to him. He stood up and closed them. Then he laid her back on the couch as he'd promised and showed her exactly what he'd wanted to do with her there the night before.

Afterward, Frannie held him and stroked his hair. Burnett told himself that though the moment of truth would come eventually, he didn't give a damn about that. Now he could hold her and love her and pretend this joy would never end.

They showered again, and then went out to the front yard, where Burnett shoveled the walk and Frannie built a snowman and they ended up throwing snow-balls like children. When Frannie hit him in the face with one, he chased her around to the back of the house and brought her down by the back fence. There they wrestled, laughing, in the snow.

Soon enough, three o'clock arrived, and it was time for dinner at Aunt Bonnie's house. Frannie wore a red wool dress and Burnett his new red shirt.

Bonnie surprised both of them by keeping her promise and behaving with charming civility. She and Frannie exchanged gifts and then her guests began to arrive. Bonnie actually urged Frannie to introduce him to her friends.

After a few minutes shaking hands and murmuring modest hellos, Burnett wandered into the kitchen. He struck up a conversation with one of the ladies he'd seen in the church the night before and was actually beginning to relax enough to enjoy himself when Frannie grabbed his arm and towed him through a short hall into the living room at the front of the house.

"Ned, I want you to meet my dad's favorite teacher, Marlon Everly. Mr. Everly!" she called.

And Burnett looked toward the front door to see the old man he'd met yesterday at the phone kiosk turning in response to his name.

Chapter Fourteen

Burnett experienced a dropping sensation in his stomach as he watched the old man toddle toward them. There was a pleasant, rather innocuous smile on the creased face, a smile belied by the alertness in the slightly watery eyes. Frannie introduced them, explaining to Burnett, "Mr. Everly taught my dad and Aunt Bonnie in school."

"So we meet again, son," the old man cackled—a little too gleefully, Burnett thought. "How's the world of high finance?"

"Fine," Burnett answered, taking the veiny extended hand. "Just fine."

"High finance?" Frannie asked.

"Little private joke." Marlon Everly cackled some more. "I saw your young fellow over town yesterday.

He was working out some big business deal on the pay phone by Yo-Ho's."

Burnett wondered grimly how he was going to get out of this one. But, as luck would have it, he kept his mouth shut long enough that Frannie did it for him.

"Oh, I get it," she said, "When you called Burnett, right?"

"Uh, yeah. Right. You got it." He sounded like an idiot, but he was so relieved, he didn't much care. "When I called Burnett."

Frannie said to Marlon Everly, "He was talking to his boss."

Marlon Everly smiled and nodded—and then looked puzzled. "His boss?" He said the two words slowly, as if, in his mind, he were turning them, studying them from all sides.

Burnett's nervousness returned. He knew he hadn't sounded much like an employee yesterday on the phone.

Marlon, meanwhile, was squinting his rheumy eyes at Burnett and feeling beneath the breast of the old tweed jacket he wore. The veiny hands came out with a cigarette and he started to put it to his lips. "Your boss? Hmm..."

From across the room, Bonnie commanded, "Marlon Everly, don't you dare light that smelly thing in my living room!"

The old man looked over his shoulder. "Now Bonnie—"

"Outside with that. I mean it." Bonnie's face wore one of her tight little frowns.

Marlon turned back to Frannie and Burnett and shrugged. "Smokers have no rights anymore. The world is not what it used to be. Excuse me." He moved toward the door, and Burnett allowed himself to relax once more.

The rest of the afternoon and evening Burnett simply avoided Marlon Everly, and the subject of what he'd really been doing on the phone the day before never came up again.

There was only one other incident of note, to Burnett's mind.

Some time after the huge turkey dinner had been eaten, and before the pies were served, the phone rang. They were all in the living room, and Bonnie went to the kitchen to get it. In a few moments she returned.

"It's your mother," Bonnie said to Frannie, her expression so noncommittal that it was almost comical.

"Thank you," Frannie said, her face as blank as her aunt's.

Frannie rose from the seat beside Burnett and disappeared into the other room. When she returned a few minutes later, Burnett gave her a questioning look. "Is anything wrong?"

Frannie counterfeited a smile. "Oh no, no. She just called to wish me a Merry Christmas."

Burnett thought then that perhaps Ned St. Charles wasn't the only one keeping secrets.

Later that night, after making long and tender love, they lay side by side in Frannie's bed upstairs, talking about the evening and Aunt Bonnie's friends.

Frannie told Burnett that Marlon Everly had been one of the town's favorite high school teachers, until his retirement several years ago. For a while after that, he'd been a substitute teacher. Now he was working on a "novel of murder and suspense" because, he used to tell his students, "The vagaries of human nature have always fascinated me."

Marlon had certain eccentricities. He refused to even consider giving up his "smokes," and he had never owned a phone in his life. He made all his calls from the pay phones in town.

"He's a sweet old guy," Frannie concluded. "My dad always admired him. My father loved to read, and he always said that Marlon Everly was most of the reason why. Marlon had a way of making the world of the printed page come alive, my dad said. I used to look forward to being old enough to be in Mr. Everly's English class."

Burnett canted up on an elbow and looked down into her eyes. "You were a daddy's girl all the way, weren't you?"

Frannie laughed. "It's that obvious, huh?"

He traced the delicate, winged shape of her collarbone with a finger. "No more obvious than the nose on your face."

"My dad was good. A good man. A helpful man, with an aura of, I don't know, warmth and contentment about him. When he died, it seemed like my whole world turned dark and lonely."

He kissed the tip of her nose. "And you've never forgiven your mother for rushing off to Tulsa like that, for taking you away from everything familiar just when you felt you needed familiar things most?"

"Partly." The word was bleak. "But it's more than that." She stirred in his arms, fitfully. "Oh, Ned. It's all in the past. And there are so many more pleasant things we could talk about. Let's just let it go for now."

He shook his head, holding her close against his side, so she couldn't turn away. "What we're supposed to be doing, remember, is getting to know all about each other?" A little pang of guilt pierced him, since all he'd told her about himself was more or less a lie. But he continued anyway, ignoring the pang, digging for the source of her pain when she spoke of her mother. "I want to understand, Angel," he said. "I want to *know* you, as much as one person can know another. And the way for me to do that is for you to share with me all that makes you who you are."

He fell silent, then, looking into her eyes, wondering with half his mind where he—Burnett Clinton, who always froze up like an iceberg when it came to intimate talk—had ever found such tender words, wondering if they were his words at all, or if perhaps they were Ned's.

Frannie said, "It's all kind of complicated."

"It's okay," he coaxed. "I can handle it."

"I mean it's *confusing*."

"Come on, Angel. Just tell me."

"Oh, all right. The truth is, my dad wasn't my real father. My *stepfather* is."

"Huh?" Burnett pulled away a little.

"I told you." She made a groaning noise. "I hate even trying to explain it. It's like some...comedy of errors, or something. And it's my life."

Burnett repeated what she'd said, trying to make it make sense. "You father wasn't your father?"

"Right. See, my mother was pregnant with me when she married the man I thought was my father. She was pregnant by a man from her hometown, who was already married."

"The man who eventually became your stepfather, you mean?"

"Yes. She ran away to California when she found out she was pregnant. She met Stanley Lawry and he knew she was pregnant, but he wanted to marry her anyway. She agreed, and for ten years the three of us were a family. And then when my dad died, she took me and went back to Tulsa, because my natural father's wife had died by then, too."

"And so, by then, your natural father was willing to marry your mother?"

"Yes. They got married, and they had more daughters. My sisters. It should have all been fine. I mean, it all worked out, didn't it? After over ten years, he finally made it legal with her. Except that to me, he's just not my father. To me, Stanley Lawry is my father. Stanley Lawry left everything he had to me. And he was there for me from the beginning.

"And worst of all," Frannie said, "she never told me. I had to find it out for myself, when she took me to Oklahoma and introduced me to a stranger and I saw my own eyes looking back at me. I ran away right after that. They brought me back. And *then,* when it was too late to mean anything, she told me the truth.''

Frannie cuddled into his shoulder, and confessed the rest. ''She wanted me to forget all about our life in California. She said Tulsa was my home now. I didn't argue with her, but in my heart, Tulsa was never home to me. She talked at first about my natural father adopting me, but she dropped that soon enough when I told her that she would never see me again if she tried something like that. I waited until I was eighteen, and then I came back to California and have stayed here ever since.

''My mother and I keep in touch, with calls at Christmas and presents through the mail. But we've never been close since then. I just don't really trust her anymore, I guess.''

Frannie laughed, a little raggedly, the sound muffled by his shoulder. ''I love her, I do. We're just not close.''

''Does your aunt know?''

''Does she ever.'' Frannie sighed and rolled onto her back. ''After I left Kenneth, she and I finally talked about it.''

''And?''

''She was relieved to have it out in the open. In fact, since then she takes every opportunity she gets to try to talk me into spending more time with my mother. See, Aunt Bonnie suspected from the first that her brother wasn't my father, because I came along only six months after they were married. They hadn't even *known* each other long enough for him to be my natural father. But Aunt Bonnie never challenged my mother about it or

anything. Aunt Bonnie's bossy, but she's got a lot of
tolerance, really. Once she saw that my mother treated
my dad well, she let it be. And, also, Aunt Bonnie felt
the way I did, that in the ways that matter, Stanley
Lawry was my dad. To her, I'm her niece just as much
as if we shared the same genes.''

Burnett found he was feeling great sympathy for
Frannie's erring mother. Probably because he understood too well that he had a lot in common with her:
both of them had trouble telling difficult truths.

He said, ''You know, you might try to see it from
your mother's point of view. Maybe she could never
quite figure out how to tell you the truth. Maybe what
she was really trying hardest to do was not to hurt you,
or lose your love.''

''Well, I can see that. I can. But she did hurt me—
much worse than if she'd been honest. And...I do still
love her.'' Frannie's voice was sad and distant. ''She
lied, that's all, for the first ten years of my life. About
something that meant the world to me. I guess that's
one thing I just have a hard time with. That someone I
love and trust could lie to me about what matters
most.''

Though Frannie spoke gently, her words hit Burnett
as if they were stones. He felt bone-weary, suddenly,
and trapped by his own deceptions. The more his angel revealed to him of the secrets of her heart, the more
he believed that there was no way she could possibly
continue loving him once she knew who he really was.

Two things she rejected: liars and domineering men.
He filled the bill on both counts.

''Ned?'' she whispered against his shoulder.

"What is it, Angel?"

"I didn't want to go into all that. But I'm glad I did. I'm glad you know."

He made a vague noise of agreement and settled her close against him.

"Tired?" she asked, her own voice soft and drowsy.

"Um." He closed his eyes and drifted off to a place of velvet darkness, a place of peace, where lies were unnecessary and his angel loved him as he really was.

Somehow, Monday arrived without his telling her the truth.

She walked him out to his Jeep in the predawn hours, down the frozen stones of the walkway that he had shoveled free of snow on Christmas Day. Her wild hair was still tangled from sleep, and she wore her red coat over a heavy flannel nightgown. She held tight to his arm, her body warm and soft against his.

Beyond the gate, beside the Jeep, they embraced and shared a long, slow kiss that was all the sweeter because they knew they would soon be apart.

He pulled away reluctantly. "I could be back as early as tonight. At the latest, I'll be here New Year's Eve. And if something comes up, I'll call your aunt's house."

Her voice had a frantic edge to it when she spoke. "I wish you would leave me a number, Ned. I don't like this. I have no way to reach you."

He felt like a jerk. Back in the house, she'd chided him again about driving without his license. "What if something happens?" she reproached him. "They won't even know who you are." He'd made soothing noises in response, quieting her fears, all the time knowing that he did have his license, right in his back pocket. And that what the license said was he was not the man she thought he was.

He cupped her sweet face in his hands. "Angel. I will call. I promise. Please believe me."

"I don't like it," she said again. Her breath came out on a silver plume, just as it had that first evening when she'd found him in the snow.

The memory of seeing her that first time pierced his heart, because it reminded him that their magical time together, one way or another, was coming to a close. Even if he never told her the truth about himself, the real world would interfere. They would both return to their day-to-day lives in Sacramento soon enough. And the fabric of deception he'd woven for her would unravel of itself, much too flimsy a thing to hold up under the hard use of everyday life.

"Please, Angel," he told her, his voice a hoarse thread that had to fight its way around the tightness in his throat. "I know I haven't made everything clear. I know it isn't fair to you. But I swear, one way or another, I'll come back before New Year's. And we'll get all this straightened out. I'll . . . tell you everything I've been holding back. There'll be nothing but honesty between us. I promise you."

She smiled then, her angel's smile. "Why is it I believe you?" she asked, as she'd asked on the night she'd agreed he could stay until Christmas.

He answered as before. "Because, about this, I'm telling the absolute truth."

And he was, he realized. When he returned, the first thing he'd do would be to explain everything, though he was almost certain he would lose her then. But he'd had his heavenly Christmas with his angel at his side. And now it was time to come back to earth. Better she hear it from him, than to find out some other way, whatever the cost.

Her light-within-dark eyes gazed into his. "I wasn't going to say this again, until you said it first."

He wanted to hear it. "Tell me."

"I love you, Ned St. Charles."

He opened his mouth to give the words back to her. But then he thought, *No. Damned if it will be Ned who'll say those words first.*

He whispered, "I'm glad."

The light in her eyes dimmed for a moment, but she kept her smile in place. "Come back to me."

"I swear it."

He kissed her once more and then climbed into the Jeep.

Chapter Fifteen

Frannie stood to watch him drive away, hugging her elbows against the cold. The Jeep started with difficulty, and when he pulled away from the sidewalk, he had to drive up to the bend that led out of town toward Reno to turn around.

It was a torment for her, to watch the Jeep disappear around the corner and then reappear a moment later. She waved, forcing a smile, as he went by once more, crossing the bridge and vanishing at the turn to Main Street.

Frannie had a terrible premonition, then. For a moment she was absolutely positive that she would never see Ned St. Charles again. But then she shook herself and told herself she was being ridiculous, letting her unfounded fears get the better of good sense.

The basis of love always had to be trust. Ned still had secrets he was keeping from her, she knew that. But he'd sworn he would explain everything when he returned. Because she loved him, she would trust what he'd told her. He *would* return, and he would explain everything then.

Straightening her shoulders, she hurried back to the warmth of her house.

When she entered the kitchen, the clock on the wall said just past four. She considered going back upstairs to try to sleep a few more hours. But she knew that would be futile. She was too keyed up. Besides, if she went up there and slipped beneath the sheets, all she'd do would be to mourn the absence of Ned's body curled around hers.

So she brewed up a pot of coffee and sat at the table and thought about the miracle that had happened to her. She reminded herself once more that soon enough, Ned would return. All the mysteries would be cleared up.

And she was sure that then he would tell her he loved her. Something—perhaps having to do with those last secrets he had yet to reveal—was holding him back from saying it aloud. But she was positive she'd seen it in his eyes. Felt it in his kiss. And experienced it in the hungry touch of his hands on her skin.

And when he returned, he would say it. She knew that, as she knew that the slight graying of the blackness beyond the windows meant dawn was on its way.

She thought, too, as she sat there watching the daylight come, of all she'd learned from him. Of the things he'd helped her see about herself and who she was.

And she thought of what he'd said about her mother: *Maybe she could never quite figure out how to tell you the truth. Maybe what she was really trying hardest to do was not to hurt you, or lose your love...*

Seen in that light, her mother's actions suddenly lost their selfish cruelty. Frannie still did not consider what her mother had done to be *right*. But she started to wonder if her mother's wrongness really mattered anymore, now that Frannie herself was no longer a grieving, confused little girl.

And then there was Kenneth. In talking about him with Ned, Frannie had been able to actually feel sorry for him, to pity him his inability to really love another person. She'd been a scared little girl still looking for her lost father with Kenneth. But since the night she'd decided to let Ned stay, she hadn't once heard Kenneth's castigating voice in her mind. She didn't need him anymore, not even his imaginary voice, to help her decide how to run her life.

Smiling to herself, Frannie went into the bathroom and took a long, hot shower. Then she made herself some hot cereal and toast, and sat down for breakfast.

When her meal was done, it was just past nine o'clock. She'd made up her mind about something while she ate, so she put on her jacket and went out the side door.

"So. He's gone," Bonnie said when she answered her door.

Frannie nodded. "He'll be back for New Year's."

"Well, don't stand there in the cold until your boots freeze to the porch. Come on in."

"Thanks, Aunt Bonnie." Frannie went inside. "Would it be all right if I used your phone? It's a long-distance call, but I'll pay you back."

Bonnie gestured toward the kitchen. "Help yourself."

Not giving herself any time to back out, Frannie went straight to the old phone on the wall and dialed her mother's number in Oklahoma.

Her youngest sister, Adele, answered the phone.

"Frannie?" Adele sounded completely disbelieving. "You okay?"

"I'm fine, Adele. Just calling to, um, say hello."

"But it's no special day, just Monday. Not Christmas or anything," Adele murmured, stymied. Then, "You *sure* you're all right?"

"I'm fine. Really." Strange, Frannie thought, how awkward it was, trying to talk to her own sister, since she'd spent so many years keeping everyone in Tulsa at a safe, polite distance.

"You want to talk to Mom?"

"In a minute, yes. But first, tell me how you've been."

Adele was silent. At last she said, "Fine."

"Are you still playing, um, football?"

"Soccer. I play soccer. And yeah. I'm playing forward this year."

"You enjoy it?"

"Yeah," Adele answered in a tone that told Frannie she really ought to come up with an intelligent question soon—or stop wasting her sixteen-year-old sister's valuable time.

"Okay, Adele," Frannie laughed. "You can put Mom on now."

"Just a minute," Adele said. Then she put the handset slightly away from her mouth and bellowed, "Mom!"

After a moment her mother's voice asked anxiously, "Frannie? Is that you?"

"Yes, Mom."

"You're all right?"

"Fine, Mom. I just, well, I realize I haven't really been keeping in touch with you. I, um, missed you, and I thought I'd call and tell you..."

"Yes?"

"I love you, Mom."

There was a silence from the other end of the line.

"Mom, are you there?"

"I'm here. And I love you, too, honey. Very much."

"I'd like to come visit, maybe during spring break, if that would be okay—"

"That would be wonderful." Her mother's voice was eager, lighter suddenly. "I would love that. *We* would love that. We truly would."

"Okay, great. We'll call it a date."

"Yes. A date," Alicia Lawry Anderson said.

There was another silence.

"Mom?"

"Yes, honey?"

"Is Father there?"

"Yes," her mother answered in a voice so full of hope, it almost broke Frannie's heart. "Yes, it just so happens he is." She rushed on, explaining what didn't need to be explained, "Would you believe it, he's down with a cold? Isn't that wonderful—I mean, well, since you called and all . . . Oh, what is wrong with me? You hang on. I'll get him."

Frannie waited. At last the deep, reticent voice said, "Hello, Frannie."

She talked to him for only a few moments, exchanging pleasantries and promising him, as she had her mother, that she would come for a visit in the spring.

At the end, her mother came back on the line briefly. "Oh, honey," she said. "I am so glad you called . . ."

Frannie said she was, too, and then they said goodbye.

She looked up to see her aunt in the doorway.

"Well," Bonnie said. "Looks to me like my favorite niece is finally *really* growing up."

"It was about time," Frannie said.

"You'll get no argument from me on that," her aunt responded.

After that, they sat in Bonnie's kitchen and Frannie drank more coffee and Bonnie allowed that sometimes, on a Monday like this, she missed her job down at the courthouse. She'd retired just a year before.

"And that's why," Bonnie went on, "I always keep a few projects on a back burner, for days like today, when I don't want to be sitting around staring at the wall, feeling old and useless."

Frannie, who'd been wondering how she was going to fill the hours that stretched out like a wasteland without Ned at her side, asked immediately, "So what's the project for today?"

"Painting the guest room upstairs. Want to help?"

Frannie jumped at the chance. In half an hour, she and Bonnie were upstairs spreading butter-colored latex on the walls.

The paint job took up half the day. And after that, Frannie returned to her house and cleaned a few closets. Then, since Bonnie had invited her, she went back over there for dinner.

From the moment Ned drove away until she finally fell asleep alone in her bed, Frannie kept herself busy. Still she found herself wondering over and over what Ned was doing now....

At twelve-thirty that afternoon, Burnett and Leland Fairgrove were washing their hands in the restroom of the Sutter Club, where Sacramento's most successful businessmen regularly went for lunch.

"I got the advertising people in on this," Leland said. "They've worked up a nice little piece to send over to the *Bee*. Do you want to take a look at it?"

Burnett took a snow-white towel from the little shelf above the basin and dried his hands, deciding that the last thing he wanted to do today was read about the franchise deal. He'd just spent the entire morning talking about it in detail. After lunch they would return to Leland's offices and, he fervently hoped, it would finally be time to put his name on the dotted line.

"Have you seen it?" Burnett asked about the work the PR firm had done.

"You bet. It's terrific." Leland smoothed his hair.

"Fine. Then approve it." Burnett tossed his towel in the bin. "And let's get back to the table, before Jordan runs off with the waitress and we *never* get that damned thing signed."

"They'll have a photographer there this afternoon," Leland said from behind him as they went through the doors to the hall. "Just a shot or two, of you and Jordan and myself while the agreement's being signed."

"Fine, no problem," Burnett said, eager to get it all over and done. They hurried to their table in the dining room upstairs. There Jordan, true to form, was ordering champagne for a beautiful woman across the room and planning where they'd go to celebrate when their business was concluded.

At a little after two, they at last returned to Fairgrave and Associates. But Jordan still wasn't satisfied with the wording of the agreement. Though this was only a preliminary document aimed at reassuring the man responsible for twelve precise locations, Jordan wanted it to say that all of southern California, Arizona and New Mexico would be franchised out through him and his group.

"Come on, Jordan," Burnett said, "that wasn't what we talked about and you know it damn well."

Jordan gave one of his famous guileless smiles. "Well, hey, Clinton. Let's talk about it now."

Leland asked his secretary for two aspirins and some spring water—and the negotiations began all over again.

It was well after six when Jordan finally agreed to accept the title of Franchise Coordinator for Chilly Lilly's Inc. That would give him the leeway to approach potential franchise owners—with the stipulation that after preliminary proposals, he would get an okay from Burnett before proceeding further.

Even Leland was happy with this solution. Everybody won. Burnett lost none of his control over his company—and yet Jordan was within his rights to warm up new franchise buyers on his own. For every buyer Jordan found—and Burnett approved—Jordan would get a nice cut of the buy-in fee.

The PR photographer set up the shot, and Burnett signed the agreement, with a beaming Jordan and Leland at his side.

"Now we celebrate," Jordan announced. "How about Frank Fat's for dinner? And then maybe over to Dawson's. And after that, who knows?"

Burnett almost said no. He wanted to see Frannie. Since leaving her, he'd felt on edge. He wanted to go back to his big empty house, put on the jeans and shirt that she had bought him, and return to the mountains where she waited for him. He wanted to hold her and kiss her once more—before he revealed the hardest truth of all.

But then he thought of how Jordan had rearranged his schedule just because Burnett had asked him to. It seemed that the least he could do was buy the man dinner to show his appreciation. And Burnett also knew he should spend tomorrow at his own office, to check that everything was going well. And then there was his nephew, Mike, who had saved a gift for him wrapped in three kinds of paper.

Jordan McSwain was grinning at him. "Well, what do you say, buddy?"

"Okay, Jordan. Let's go celebrate."

* * *

In Downieville, Tuesday dawned clear and bright.

Frannie's second cousin, Andy, came over and asked her if she wanted to go up to the summit and ride snowmobiles. She went, crammed between Andy and his wife and their two daughters, in the cab of their big pickup truck.

They rode the motor-driven sleds in the deep, powdery snow, and ate lunch off the bed of the trailer on which the sleds had been towed up the steep and winding road.

They didn't come home until almost dark, riding down from Sierra City, packed tight in the cab, singing rock and roll songs from the fifties at the top of their lungs and laughing when they forgot what line came next.

Frannie felt anticipation building as they approached the limits of town. There was a rising feeling in her throat, an excitement and an expectant joy.

What if Ned were there when she arrived at her house? Or what if he'd called Aunt Bonnie?

She tried not to indulge her disappointment when neither possibility turned out to be true. She watched her aunt's favorite game show with her, and then returned to her own house, where she discovered her nose was sunburned—and the fires were both cold.

Stomping down to the freezing basement to get more wood, she realized she'd grown spoiled having Ned with her. She hadn't even thought about the fires while he had stayed in her house.

She tucked herself in early, cuddling up with a novel of romantic suspense. She read the whole thing before she fell asleep, because she just didn't like sleeping without Ned at her side anymore.

In Sacramento, Burnett went through his mail and got a rundown from his secretary. Everything at Chilly Lilly's Inc. had been going along fine.

He went to his brother's for dinner, where he passed out the gifts he'd rushed around in the afternoon buying. He received his present from his nephew—a computer game called Combat Chess, at which Mike promptly slaughtered him.

After Mike went to bed, and Joanna, an artist, disappeared into her studio, Casey wanted to know how things had gone with *the angel*.

"I'm going back tomorrow, for New Year's."

"Did you tell her the truth?"

"Not yet."

"Not good, Big Brother."

"I know."

"Well then?"

"I'll tell her tomorrow."

"Good."

Burnett went to the big French doors that looked out on the pool. "I don't know, Casey," he said, staring at his own shadowy reflection in the glass of the door. "I'm afraid I'll lose her the minute I tell her."

"It's a risk," Casey reluctantly agreed from behind him. "But it'll be a hell of a lot worse if she finds out from somebody else."

"I know," Burnett said, turning back to the spacious room. "How about another Scotch and soda?"

"Help yourself."

* * *

Wednesday morning in Downieville, Frannie looked out her window on a gunmetal sky. Another storm was on the way.

She rose and fed the fires and decided to go over to the Downieville Bakery, on the other side of the bridge, for her morning coffee and a sweet roll. She just wasn't in the mood to have breakfast alone—especially when she knew she could be snowed in by noon.

She pulled on a heavy blue sweater and some jeans, and tucked her hair beneath a big cashmere tam that her mother had sent her in the mail Christmas before last. Wearing the matching scarf and her red jacket, she went out into the gray, blustery morning. She paused at her front gate to wrap her scarf closer about her and turn her collar up. Then she started down the street, pushing against the harsh wind all the way.

The bakery, housed in the historic Craycroft building, which also contained Yo-Ho's store, was doing a brisk business when Frannie arrived. She got in line in the small area where the glass cases displayed doughnuts and sweet rolls and muffins and such. After her turn to order came, she took her coffee and the paper-lined basket containing a huge apple fritter into the adjacent dining room.

She saw Marlon Everly immediately. He sat at a table in the corner. There was a cup of coffee at his elbow, and he puffed on one of his ever-present cigarettes. Before him was a newspaper, which he appeared to be scanning with extreme avidity.

Frannie hesitated for a moment before joining him. He looked completely absorbed in his paper. But she really did want to chat with someone, to share a little neighborly conversation before she returned to the house to wait out the storm. And Marlon Everly seemed capable enough of speaking up if he wanted to be alone.

She strolled over to him. "Want some company, Mr. Everly?"

His head jerked up. "Eh?" He narrowed his eyes at her. "Frannie!" he said—and then quickly folded the paper over on itself. "Please. Have a seat."

Frannie slid into the chair beside him, wondering at his strained expression and the furtive way he seemed to be hiding the paper from her. "Is everything all right?"

"Eh? Certainly. Everything is fine."

"You look so... strange, Mr. Everly."

He chuckled. "Well, I am strange, child. Anyone who lives to be past eighty tends to get a little strange."

Frannie wasn't buying. "What are you reading?"

"Hmm? Eh?"

"In the paper? Is there something in the paper?"

"Something?" he asked, sounding like a bad recording. "In the paper? Why..."

Frannie looked at him. And he looked back. And then he shrugged and took another puff from his cigarette. He lifted his arm off the newspaper and pushed it over in front of her.

Frannie looked down at the paper. And then she gave a nervous, unconvincing laugh. What in the world could be in there that would make Marlon Everly behave so oddly?

Frannie flipped open the paper. She saw that it was the Metro section of the *Sacramento Bee*. She also saw a color photograph of Ned.

Frannie blinked. But when she opened her eyes again, the picture was still there. In it, Ned was shaking hands with a big blond man while a thin, serious fellow looked on. All three men were immaculately dressed.

The caption read: Ice-Cream King Closes Sweet Deal.

"You must understand, my dear," Marlon Everly was murmuring in an apprehensive tone. "You introduced him as...Ned, wasn't it? And just now, you surprised me. When I looked up and saw you, my first instinct was to protect you, because I thought perhaps you didn't know..."

Frannie didn't look up. She couldn't take her eyes off the picture. She was trying desperately to assimilate what such a thing might mean. A picture of her raggedy man, all dressed up in a fine suit. Looking supremely comfortable, utterly confident. Looking distant and domineering.

A man just like Kenneth had been. The kind of man she had sworn never to get anywhere near, ever again.

"Frannie?" Marlon Everly's voice came at her, sounding extremely concerned.

Frannie ignored him. She looked at the caption beneath the picture of Ned and read:

Burnett Clinton, Owner and President of Chilly Lilly's, Inc.

Frannie's mind seemed to have gone numb. She had to strain to comprehend what she saw, what the picture and the words on the paper were trying to tell her.

That Ned was not Ned.

That Ned was the man he had said was his boss.

Burnett Clinton was Ned.

And, in reality, there *was* no Ned. Had never been a Ned. It had all been some awful, cruel, incredible joke...

"Frannie, my dear, are you all right?" Marlon Everly was asking.

Frannie looked up, and made herself smile. It would not be a good idea to break down here, she decided with the part of her mind that continued to function. Not here, in the bakery, with everyone looking on. It simply wouldn't do, as Aunt Bonnie would say.

"Mr. Everly?" Frannie asked brightly. "May I take this paper?"

"Why certainly you may. Of course. But are you sure you're—"

Frannie stood up, clutching the paper against her breast. "I'm fine. Just fine. Only surprised. You're right, you see. I didn't know."

Marlon Everly reached for his cane. "Allow me to walk with you."

Frannie understood his concern. She knew she probably didn't look as "fine" as she insisted she was. "No. Please. I really am all right. I just need ... I need to be by myself right now."

"Are you sure?"

"Positive."

Marlon Everly reluctantly sank back to his seat. "All right, my dear. If you're sure . . ."

Frannie gave him another forced, wide smile and scooted free of the table and got out of there. She raced across the bridge, the fierce wind at her back. The storm had begun, an angry storm, one that tore at her scarf and stung her cheeks with sleeting snow.

When she reached the partial haven of her porch, she yanked off her boots and went in the side door. She sat down at the kitchen table without even removing her coat or her tam and scarf.

She spread the paper open on the table, and then, very slowly, she read every word of the article that accompanied the picture.

It said that Burnett Clinton had taken a single ice-cream store owned by his family and turned it into a million-dollar corporation. It said that after this franchising operation was successfully completed, Chilly Lilly's Inc.—and Burnett Clinton—would have doubled the number of stores in the chain, and massively increased his company's net worth.

And to Frannie Lawry, it said that she'd fallen for another wheeler-dealer. And one much worse than Kenneth. Kenneth, at least, had never pretended to be other than he was.

Outside the wind and sleet beat against the windows. Frannie was hardly aware of the storm. She sat for a measureless time, staring at the picture that showed the complete and total betrayal of the man she'd allowed herself to love.

She didn't hear the tapping on the side door. Finally her Aunt Bonnie had to let herself in.

"Marlon called me," Bonnie said when she stood beside the table. "He was worried about you."

Frannie looked up into her aunt's round face. "You were right, Aunt Bonnie. You were right all along." She pushed the paper over, nearer where her aunt stood.

Bonnie looked down at it, scanned it at a glance. Then she looked up at Frannie again, those dark eyes that could be so sharp, soft with tender sympathy.

"He lied," Frannie said. "About everything."

For once Bonnie Lawry said nothing. She removed her coat and hung it on the hook by the door. Then she returned to the table and sat down. She scooted her chair next to Frannie's, and put her arms around her niece. At first Frannie stiffened, then she sagged against her aunt's solid strength.

Frannie felt her aunt's hands, removing the tam, pulling loose the scarf, and then cradling her close again, stroking her hair. Frannie sighed.

Bonnie spoke at last. "You'll feel better if you cry."

"I can't."

"It's no good holding it back."

"I'm not. I'm just...numb. I can't cry right now."

Bonnie continued to stroke her hair.

"I don't know," Frannie said in a flat voice against her aunt's substantial bosom, "if he'll even come back."

"Oh, he'll be back," Bonnie said.

"What do you know about it, Aunt Bonnie?"

"I know enough," Bonnie replied.

"I won't see him."

"You'll see him."

Frannie sighed. "Aunt Bonnie, I get so tired of arguing with you."

"I'm not arguing, Frances. I'm just stating the facts."

Chapter Sixteen

The sky overhead was dangerously dark when Burnett started for Downieville at 8:00 a.m. It rained on and off up through Auburn, and the rain became snow as he neared Grass Valley.

But the real storm caught him after he'd left Nevada City, at the middle fork of the Yuba River just as he crossed the bridge there. It was nothing like the storms he'd known during the days he spent with his angel. Those had been windless, gentle things, where the snow drifted down thick and soft to cover everything in a pristine blanket of white.

This was a blowing, sleety gale of a storm. The snow came at the windshield fiercely, attacking it, pelting it as if it wanted to shatter the glass. He had to slow to a crawl for safety's sake, though the old Jeep did have all-weather tires.

As he climbed the last—and highest—hill before descending into the final canyon and crossing the bridge over the north fork of the Yuba, the sleeting snow became so thick that he could see it building up on the road. Even his snow tires weren't holding. He was afraid he was going to have to pull over and put on the ancient chains that were stored underneath the seat.

But then, behind him, he saw the powerful, beacon-like headlights. And he heard the scraping of the pavement, even through the howling of the storm. It was the snowplow.

Carefully he veered to the side when he found a wide space. He let the plow go by. Then he followed it, traveling at a snail's pace, but safely, for the final fifteen miles.

It took nearly an hour, but he arrived at the point above Downieville without incident. The snowplow turned out at the wide space in the road there, moving in a circle, and then heading back the way it had come.

He waved at the driver. Then he slowly started down into the small valley, where the town lay sleeping, closed in on itself against the wildness of the storm.

"Drink your hot milk," Bonnie instructed.

Frannie obediently lifted the cup to her lips and took a sip. They were sitting in the living room, where Bonnie had sent her after helping her out of her coat. Bonnie had heated the milk, and then joined her here in front of the open fireplace.

"I'm going to be fine, Aunt Bonnie. Really I am."

"Of course you are."

Frannie set her cup aside. She still felt numb. Nothing seemed real. But she was conscious of a vague surprise at the way her aunt was behaving.

"I thought you'd be ranting and raving by now, about him," Frannie said.

"No sense locking up the barn now. The horses have gone."

"What's that supposed to mean?"

"You love him."

"I don't. I don't even know him."

"I liked him. When I got to know him."

"Aunt Bonnie. You didn't know him. He wasn't who he said he was at all."

Bonnie grew pensive. "I think he was a lot who he said he was, *whoever* it turns out he actually is."

If Frannie hadn't felt so dead inside, she might have laughed. "Aunt Bonnie, I don't know what you're talking about."

"Yes, you do, Frances. You understand me just fine."

"He's Kenneth Dayton all over again. Can't you see that?"

"Humph," Bonnie said to that. "No, I can't. I despised Kenneth Dayton from the first minute you introduced us."

"You despised Ned—I mean Burnett, too."

"Yes, I did. But the more I got to know him—"

Frannie wearily waved a hand. "That's enough. Please. I don't want to talk about it anymore."

"Well, fine. Don't cry. Don't talk. I'm sure keeping it all in will do you a world of good. I'm sure your support group would be proud of you."

"Aunt Bonnie—"

But Bonnie was gesturing toward the front window. "Well. What did I tell you? I said he'd be back."

Frannie looked where her aunt pointed. And saw Ned.

No, not Ned. There was no Ned. She saw Burnett. Burnett Clinton coming up her front steps. He seemed to be materializing out of the gale, because the storm was so fierce there was nothing but swirling white from halfway down the yard.

He wore the clothes she'd given him—the boots and jeans and heavy jacket. He held himself hunched against the cruel wind, and he stomped the snow off his boots before he approached the front door and disappeared from her line of sight.

"I'll let myself out the back," Bonnie said.

Frannie hardly heard her. All of her being, her entire self, was focused on the front door.

The knock came, three strong raps on the old brass knocker. Frannie shook herself, registering the fact that Bonnie was gone. She rose from the faded wing chair by the fire and slowly, on unresponsive feet, approached the door.

He knocked again before she got there. And that energized her. She hurried the rest of the way and flung open the door.

And then she couldn't move. She looked at him. The snow, borne on the ruthless, turbulent air, blew in the door and swirled around their feet. She ignored it.

He looked so handsome and solid, standing there in the angry wind. Some traitorous part of her wanted to open her arms to him, pull him close to her, feel his breath warm her face as she lifted her lips to offer a welcoming kiss.

But she stood firm against such dangerous desires. She watched his face, watched it change. From a look of joy and hunger, to puzzlement, to slowly dawning awareness.

In the end, he broke the silence. He said two words, "You know."

She nodded, then stepped out of the way. He entered. She closed out the storm.

"How?" he asked. "Who told you?"

She turned toward the kitchen. He followed her there.

She pointed to the newspaper. He looked at it.

Then he shoved it away, muttering a brief expletive, and sank into a chair. She sat down, as well, after moving her chair a safe distance away.

He looked at the table for a while, then he looked at her once more, his eyes pleading. "Angel—"

"Don't call me that!" The words seemed to explode out of her mouth. "Don't..." She forced herself to breathe, to get herself into some semblance of control. Then she finished with great care, "Don't ever call me that again."

"Damn it, I'm sorry," he said in a hoarse whisper.

"You're sorry." She repeated the words very softly, with utter lack of belief.

"Yes. I wanted to tell you. I tried to tell you. All along. But I knew damn well I'd lose you. Like I'm losing you now."

"Why did you do it?" she asked. "Why did you lie in the first place?"

"I wanted to be anyone that day, anyone but myself."

"St. Charles for the bar?"

"Yeah."

"And Ned? Why Ned?"

"Frannie—"

"Answer me." Her voice was rising again, getting close to going out of control. She forced it back into a flat, even tone and repeated, "You answer me now. I've got a right to the truth, after all of your lies."

"All right. Edward is my first name. I used to be called Ned, when I was a kid."

"What are you trying to make me think? That it wasn't *really* a lie, since Ned *is* your real name?"

"I'm not trying to make you think anything." He sounded tired, beaten. "You asked and I told you."

"Why should I believe you?"

He peered at her very closely then, and she wondered in a strange, scared way, what he saw. He said, "You told me you loved me. If you do—"

She couldn't bear to hear more. She threw up a hand. "I loved *Ned*, remember? Not some stranger. Not you."

His face tightened, as if she'd struck him. "You said you loved me." He spoke so low she barely heard it beneath the howling of the wind.

"No!" The word was ugly, raw with pain. "You're not Ned. You're a fake and a liar. You...you made love with me under false pretenses. You let me think you were somebody I could trust, somebody I could count on, somebody...*real*."

"I *am* real."

She loosed an ugly short laugh. "You? Real? You're not real. You're just—"

Something seemed to snap in him then. He raised his bent head. "What?" Now his face was expressionless.

"Just—" Frannie cut herself off this time. His dark eyes looked dangerous. She realized she had probably gone too far. "Never mind," she said. "What counts is, it's over."

He stood up. "Oh, really?" He wore that distant look now, the one that he'd worn when he'd posed for the picture in the paper.

She stood up, too, not wanting to have him look down on her. "Yes, it's over." She thought her voice sounded very calm. She congratulated herself on that. Because she didn't feel calm.

Something had happened. Everything had shifted. He'd been behaving like Ned might have, trying to get through to her, to make her understand. But then, at some point, he'd decided he wasn't going to get through to her. He'd given up on being vulnerable. He'd put up stone walls around his emotions. Frannie feared what he might say—or do—next.

"Why is it over?" he asked, still in that distant, coldly curious voice.

Frannie felt outraged that he would even ask such a question. She let her anger show. "What do you mean, why? You're the kind of man I never want anything to do with again. And everything you told me about yourself was a lie."

"I admit I lied," he said.

"And you think that makes everything all right?"

"I lied at first," he went on patiently, "because I was drunk and too out of it to know better. And I kept on lying for an understandable reason."

"What reason?"

"Because I knew you'd kick me out if I told you the truth. Pretending to be Ned was the only way to get close to you."

"I should have kicked you out," she said. "I *would* have kicked you out, you're right. And I would have been entirely justified."

"My point exactly." He stepped toward her. She shrank back. "Ned was the only chance I had with you. I took it. And damned if I'll regret it now." He reached out for her, and pulled her close against him.

Frannie gasped at the sweet fire that coursed through her veins at the feel of his big body against hers. He was bad for her, wrong for her. Yet she still wanted him. She was shamed.

"You wanted me," he said into her flushed face. "You still want me. By any name."

"Let me go."

Immediately he released her. Her knees felt weak. She forced herself not to lean against the back of the chair.

He said, "You used Ned, as much as I did."

"That's absurd," she shot back, her voice suddenly wavering, her throat going dry.

"You're afraid of losing control," he went on, merciless now. "You have some confused idea that any strong man will walk all over you. But you were attracted to me. You wanted me. And as long as I was weak, as long as you knew you could dominate me, you could give yourself permission to desire me, to go to bed with me, to even call what you felt for me love.''

The words hurt, they were awful. She didn't want to hear more. ''Stop!'' she said, the sound raw and torn.

But he did nothing of the kind. ''You *liked* the idea that I had nothing, that you bought the clothes I wore, paid for the food I ate, that everything—even that Christmas gift I gave you—came from you first.'' He took a step toward her. She stepped back. ''What was I to you, really? A kind of revenge, maybe? On your precious 'Dad' for dying and leaving you so young, on your ex-husband for making you into the woman of his dreams and then replacing you without a backward glance the minute you turned out to have needs of your own?'' He took another step. Frannie didn't move back this time. She stared up into his face, horrified, mesmerized, dying inside.

''I'm not either of them, Frannie—your dad or your ex,'' he said hoarsely into her upturned face. ''And I'm also not your sweet, harmless Ned St. Charles.'' Suddenly he blinked and shook his head, and all the fury seemed to go out of him.

He said, very softly, ''Hell, I don't think I know who I am right now.''

He stepped back from her, seeming almost to fade away. ''I *am* sorry, Frannie,'' he said in a tender voice. ''I only wanted to love you, I swear. But I just never was any good at that. Not any good at all.''

She realized then that he was planning to leave, which was exactly what she wanted—a few minutes ago. He was already in the door to the dining room before she called out.

"Wait. You can't go now." Like a coward, she added lamely, "The storm..."

He shook his head. "I'll follow the plow. It's perfectly safe."

"Oh, please," she cried. He stopped. "Ned—" The word was past her lips before she remembered to hold it back.

He turned then, and looked at her. He let out a sad chuckle. "You've got the wrong guy," he said. And then he was gone.

Chapter Seventeen

Had she? Frannie wondered. Had she got the wrong guy?

She stood staring at the doorway to the dining room after he was gone from it. She heard the outside door open, allowing brief entry to the wrathful wind. And then she heard it close.

Had she got the wrong guy?

Very loud, then, someone shouted, "No!"

And she was halfway to the front door before she realized it had been herself. She raced through the dining room, and then across the front room rug to the door.

She flung open the door and shouted, "Burnett! Wait!"

But there was only the thick, spinning snow and the howling wind and—seemingly a thousand miles away—the sound of an engine starting up.

Oblivious to the cold and wind, she raced out onto the porch in her stockinged feet. "Damn you, Burnett! You get back here!"

No answer came, of course. That distant engine was pulling away. Frannie shot off the porch and into the high drifts in the yard. She struggled, pushing and fighting with all her strength, out into the thick, blind force of the storm.

Somehow she made it to the front gate. Her feet were freezing, so cold they burned. If she stayed out in this much longer, she knew, they wouldn't hurt at all. And that would be bad indeed.

But she was less than a hundred feet from her own house, she reminded herself staunchly. And all she had to do was somehow get out into the road and flag Burnett down after he went up the street to turn around. She knew she could do it. She knew she wouldn't damage her poor feet that badly, just from a few minutes out in this freezing gale.

She got the iron gate open, burning her hands on the frozen metal of it. And then she pushed on, out onto what she assumed was the sidewalk, so covered with snow now that there was no clear place where it ended and the street began.

She shielded her eyes with a hand, squinting against the storm—and made out the taillights of the Jeep just as they were swallowed by the swirling snow. It took her a moment to orient herself enough to realize what she'd seen.

This time he hadn't gone up the highway to turn around. This time he'd backed toward the bridge and turned onto Pearl Street. That meant he'd go to the end of that, turn left at the bridge there, and leave town by coming back down Main.

He'd escaped her.

And her feet were *freezing*.

She raced back to her house, floundering twice in the yard, crazily almost losing her way less than thirty feet from the front door. At last, she lumbered up the porch steps, her feet feeling like huge lead clubs attached to her aching ankles.

She fell in the door—and confronted her aunt.

"Are you insane, Frances Anne?"

Frannie dropped to the rug, tore off her sock, and began massaging one foot. Her aunt dropped down beside her, ripped off the other sock, and worked on the remaining foot.

"I could ask you the same question," Frannie muttered as she rubbed the circulation back into her toes. "You were obviously out in it, too."

"Just between the houses. In the proper clothing. What happened?"

"He left. I was trying to catch him. But he disappeared down Pearl Street. He's probably halfway up to Cannon Point by now."

"What do you intend to do?"

"Go after him. I don't even have a phone number for him. If I don't catch him on the road, I'll have to call one of his ice-cream stores or something to try to track him down."

Bonnie looked up from her concentration on Frannie's foot. "You're okay. Get over by the fire. I'll bring you dry clothes."

"Aunt Bonnie? My truck's out back, buried in the snow…"

"Yes," Bonnie answered, before Frannie even asked. "You may borrow mine. It's parked on the street out front."

An hour later, as Frannie slowly followed in a small caravan of vehicles behind a snowplow, she was forced to admit that she was never going to catch up to him. He'd had too much of a start on her.

An hour after that, when she reached the highway at Nevada City, and the storm began to abate, she considered turning back for Downieville.

Instead she veered off at Brunswick Road and found a gas station where she could call her aunt. Bonnie promised to close up the house for her, and Frannie said she'd return the truck within a few days.

Frannie drove on to Sacramento, to her two-bedroom condominium not far from the college. Once inside, she turned on the heat and brewed a pot of tea.

Then she took the snow bubble Burnett had given her from the pocket of her jacket where she'd stuck it before leaving her house in the mountains. She set it on the counter where she could see it if she faltered, and she got out the phone book.

There was no Burnett Clinton listed in the book. That didn't surprise her. She smiled to herself. He was such a big shot, after all. And big shots didn't put their names in the phone book for just anyone to dial.

She found a main office number for Chilly Lilly's Inc. When she called it, a receptionist answered. The receptionist was perfectly willing to take a number, but had no idea when Mr. Clinton might be in.

After that, Frannie sipped her tea for a few moments, refusing to let herself give up. If she had to, she'd march right over to one of his ice-cream stores. She'd chain herself to a freezer. They wouldn't be able to get rid of her until *Mr. Clinton* agreed to speak to her in person.

She racked her brain for something—anything he might have said during their time together that could provide her with a clue to how to reach him now.

And at last, something came to her. She set down her teacup, and turned the snow bubble upside down once. She stared at the somber angel within.

The brother, she thought as the swirling flakes settled. He'd said he had a brother. A brother named Casey. He'd said Casey was the wild one, who fell in love with his best friend.

And Frannie had never doubted that he was telling the truth.

Because, she decided, he *had* been telling the truth. She would bet the only thing she had left of him now— the snow bubble angel he'd bought her with her own money—that all he had told her about himself and his family had been true. That he'd altered it only enough to fit his identity as Ned.

Frannie opened the phone book again to the C's. If only he'd given her his brother's real name....

It was there. Casey Clinton, just as she'd prayed.
Now, if only *this* Casey Clinton had a brother named
Burnett.

With shaking hands, she dialed the number, hoping
fervently that someone would pick up.

Three rings, then a child's voice.

"Hello?"

"Hello—is Casey Clinton there?"

"Yes," said the child.

"May I speak to him?"

"Um, whom may I say is calling?"

Frannie smiled at the well-trained, polite little voice.
"This is Frannie, Frannie Lawry. But wait a moment—"

"Yes?"

"Are you Mike?"

"How'd you know?"

Relief coursed through Frannie, a warm, fine thing.
Mike was the nephew. Casey and Burnett had once
battled over who would have custody of him. She was
reasonably sure now that she'd reached Burnett's
brother.

But then she realized she wasn't out of the woods
yet. Casey probably had no idea who Frannie Lawry
was. She would have to convince him that he should
give her a number where his brother might be found.

"I'll get Uncle Casey," Mike was saying.

"Thank you," Frannie answered, her voice sounding faint.

"Hello, Frannie Lawry." The voice was not as deep
as Burnett's, but it was undeniably masculine. And

there was great humor in it. Frannie had a feeling she would like Burnett's brother very much.

Frannie swallowed. He'd said her name as if he knew her—or at least, knew *of* her. "You know me?" she asked in a silly little squeak.

Casey laughed. "I've heard all about you."

"From Burnett?" She knew the question was silly when she asked it, but it just came out. How else would he have heard about her?

"Yes," Casey answered, an indulgent smile in his voice, "from Burnett. Is there something I can do for you?"

Now came the hard part. "Well, um, I have a little problem."

"Yeah?"

"I seem to have lost him."

"My brother?"

"Yes. And I lost him *before* I got his phone number."

"You did?"

"He left in a blizzard, actually. I chased him out to the road."

"I see."

"But he was already gone."

"Oh."

"So I was wondering . . ."

"Yeah?"

"Do you have a number where I could get a hold of him?"

There was a silence, then Casey asked, "This is your business, I understand. But is everything all right?"

Frannie sighed. "I think maybe it will be. If I can ever *find* him to make it that way."

"Okay," Casey said. "Hold on."

He gave her two phone numbers, and addresses to go with them—for Burnett's house in Sacramento and for his private line at his office. He also explained how to get to the cabin in Graeagle, if the other two numbers turned up nothing.

"Call me back, would you?" Casey asked then. "I mean, if you can't find him."

"I will. And thank you."

Frannie hung up, and then immediately started to dial Burnett's home number. But she didn't complete the call.

She replaced the phone in its cradle. More than likely, she reasoned, he would be at home. He wouldn't have tried for Graeagle in the storm. And it was a little late in the day to be showing up at the office.

She wanted to see him. In person. She didn't want him to have a chance to shut her out on the phone.

Frannie threw on her jacket and grabbed up the keys to the truck and went out the door.

The house was a Colonial-style brick structure, set back from the road on a beautifully landscaped lot. She pulled her aunt's old truck right up into the turn-around driveway in front of a stone fountain.

Frannie stepped out of the truck, slamming the door smartly behind her. Above, the sky was still gray, though it was not raining right then. It was cold. Not as cold as in the mountains. This was a more subtle kind of cold, gray and oppressive, the kind of cold that crept into your bones.

Frannie snuggled her red jacket closer about her and marched up to the front door, which was imposingly tall and framed by white columns. She rang the bell and then waited, looking up at the chandelier above her head—an iron creation on a chain.

She began to doubt he could be inside, since he didn't answer, and she'd detected no trace of life or light through any of the paned, shuttered windows upstairs or down. But then, she thought there was a faint brightening in the window nearest the door, as if perhaps the light in the foyer had been turned on.

The door slowly swung back.

She almost expected to see a poker-faced butler standing there. But instead it was Burnett, still wearing the clothes she'd bought him, minus the boots.

They stared at each other, then he growled. "What the hell are you doing here?"

She growled right back. "I came to finish what we started."

He scowled at her for a moment. And then he stepped back and gestured her inside.

Chapter Eighteen

He led her through the domed foyer, down a wide hall and into a big living room furnished with overstuffed skirted chairs and sofas covered in floral patterns. The tables were brass and glass. The fine rugs, in muted rose-and-blue designs, only brought out the rich depth of the hardwood floor all the more. It was an elegant room—and one with a distinctly feminine touch.

Frannie hesitated in the doorway. "Amanda decorated the whole house?" she asked, reasonably sure of his answer.

"Yes."

"It's beautiful—or at least what I've seen so far is."

"It's perfect," he said, the way another person might have said, *I hate it.*

She responded to his tone, rather than his words. "You could move."

"I intend to."

"That's good."

He turned away from her then, in a quick, frustrated movement. "Damn it, Frannie . . ."

She ventured into the exquisite room, crossing the soft rugs and the smooth, shining floor. He stood by one of the tall, shuttered windows. She approached him, stopping less than an arm's distance away.

She spoke softly to his back. "Within the lie, it was all true, wasn't it?"

"Yes."

"Amanda's miscarriages, the fight over custody of Mike, all that you said about your family. You even gave me all their real names."

"Yes."

"And last Tuesday *was* the day your divorce was final, and you actually did throw your money and wallet in the river—for exactly the reason you gave me."

He nodded. "I did."

"What was in the pocket of your coat?"

"My driver's license." He gave a humorless chuckle. "Hell, I was drunk. I thought it was brilliant of me to save some identification—at the same time as I was wishing I was anyone else but myself."

"Where did you get those awful clothes?"

"Upstairs in the Graeagle cabin. It was the same thing. I found them comforting. I wanted to be someone else."

"Someone like Ned?"

"Yeah, I guess so." He turned then, and allowed himself to look at her. "I liked being Ned. At the same time as I was jealous as hell of him."

"Why?"

His eyes turned bleak and then he looked away with the slightest twist of his head. "Because you adored him."

She took the step that separated them, and laid her hand on his cheek. She guided his face back to her. "I adored him because he was you. He *is* you."

He captured her hand; his eyes now burned into hers. "You think so?"

"I know so. It was all true, what you said. I let myself be attracted to you as Ned, because you seemed to be someone who would never try to run my life. But I think deep down I knew there was much more to you. I lied to myself as much as you lied to me. I deceived myself so I could let myself love you, so I could put aside my fear of what might happen if I loved a strong man."

"And what exactly was that?"

"That you would dominate me, like you said. That what happened with Kenneth would happen all over again."

"And do you still fear that?"

"No," she answered, the word firm and sure.

"Why?"

"Two reasons. I'm not the confused, lost little girl I once was. And you are not Kenneth Dayton, not by a long shot."

"I'm not?"

"No. You're not."

"How do you know?"

"Because I know you. You revealed your real self to me, even if you cheated a little on the last name."

"I lied."

"Not really, not in your heart. Because you *are* Ned, don't you see? Ned is part of you. The vulnerable, sensitive part. The part that you buried, I think, when your father deserted your family. But you're also strong and determined and ready to take on the world. That's important, too. Otherwise, as you once told me, you would be the kind of man that no self-respecting woman would really be willing to put up with for long."

He raised her captured hand to his lips, and he kissed it very softly. Frannie felt the sweet caress along every nerve. "And when did you realize all of this?" he wondered.

"Four hours ago. When you walked out on me. You said I had the wrong guy when I called you Ned. But I didn't. I had exactly the right guy. And I knew it then. I followed you out in the storm to tell you, but you got away."

"To tell me what, specifically?" He held her hand against his heart. She felt the warmth of him, and the solid strength.

"That I love you, Edward Burnett Clinton. I love all of you, with all my heart."

He dragged in a sharp breath, and then he said softly, "Thank God."

His free arm pulled her close. His mouth closed over hers, and she clung to him, offering all of herself, letting him know with her kiss that there was no lie, no equivocation, in the things she had said.

For a time, in the flawless room there was only the sound of shared sighs.

It was he who at last reluctantly pulled away. "I wanted to tell you, since Christmas Eve, that I loved you. But I didn't want to say it..."

"When I only knew you as Ned?"

"Yes."

"And now?" she prompted.

"Now I'll say it."

"Yes?"

"I love you, Frannie Lawry."

She smiled at him. "I'm glad—and Burnett?"

"What?"

"Would it be all right, if every once in a while, I call you Ned?"

He gave a low chuckle. "Why not? If you'll still be my angel."

She thought then of the proud, sad angel he'd given her, trapped in her bubble of glittering snow. She said, "I'm no angel, Burnett."

"Sure you are," he told her, "sometimes. Just like a part of me is Ned. You are my angel." He pulled her close once more, and his lips hovered a breath's distance from hers. "And you're also much more than that."

"I'm glad you noticed."

"Oh, I've noticed..." His lips brushed hers.

"What? Tell me."

"You're a hell of a woman."

"Why thank you."

"And there are many things I'd like to call you. Frannie. Angel. Wife."

She pressed herself closer to him. "Yes," she said.

"Is that an answer?"

"Yes."

"You'll marry me?" He looked, right then, as sensitive and vulnerable as he ever had as Ned.

"Absolutely," she told him.

"Right away. Tomorrow," he said, taking charge, making demands, behaving like Burnett Clinton to the core.

Frannie reached up, wrapped her arms around his neck, and pulled his mouth down to hers.

"Yes," she said. "Now kiss me."

And he willingly complied.

They were married in Reno, on New Year's Day. Their first child, a daughter, was born a year later, on the anniversary of the day Frannie glanced out her kitchen window to see a poor, ragged man struggling up the levee in the snow.

They named their daughter Angela.

*   *   *   *   *

Silhouette Special Edition

salutes

MOMENTS OF GLORY

from Lindsay McKenna

In a country torn with conflict, in a time of bitter passions, these brave men and women wage a war against all odds... and a timeless battle for honor, for fleeting moments of glory, for the promise of enduring love.

February: RIDE THE TIGER (#721) Survivor Dany Villard is wise to the love-'em-and-leave-'em ways of war, but wounded hero Gib Ramsey swears she's captured his heart... forever.

March: ONE MAN'S WAR (#727) The war raging inside brash and bold Captain Pete Mallory threatens to destroy him, until Tess Ramsey's tender love guides him toward peace.

April: OFF LIMITS (#733) Soft-spoken Marine Jim McKenzie saved Alexandra Vance's life in Vietnam; now he needs her love to save his honor....

SEMG-1

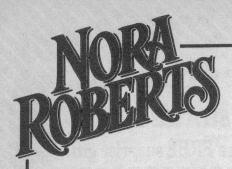

NORA ROBERTS

Love has a language all its own, and for centuries, flowers have symbolized love's finest expression. Discover the language of flowers—and love—in this romantic collection of 48 favorite books by bestselling author Nora Roberts.

Starting in February 1992, two titles will be available each month at your favorite retail outlet.

In February, look for:

Irish Thoroughbred, Volume #1
The Law Is A Lady, Volume #2

Collect all 48 titles and become fluent in the Language of Love.

LOL192

THE LANGUAGE of LOVE